PENSIERI

PENSIERI

GIACOMO LEOPARDI

TRANSLATED BY W. S. DI PIERO

A BILINGUAL EDITION

NEW YORK , OXFORD

OXFORD UNIVERSITY PRESS

OXFORD UNIVERISTY PRESS
Oxford   London   Glasgow
New York   Toronto   Melbourne   Auckland
Delhi   Bombay   Calcutta   Madras   Karachi
Kuala Lumpur   Singapore   Hong Kong   Tokyo
Nairobi   Dar es Salaam   Cape Town
and associate companies in
Beirut   Berlin   Ibadan   Mexico City   Nicosia

The edition of the *Pensieri* used in preparing this translation is from *Tutte le opere*, edited by Francesco Flora (4th edition; Milan: Mondadori, 1953).

The translation of Pensiero XX was previously published in *The Smith* as "On Writers Who Recite" and is reprinted here with the gracious permission of Harry Smith. The passage from Horace's *The Art of Poetry*, translated by Burton Raffel, quoted herein, is reprinted with the gracious permission of the State Univeristy of New York Press.

Library of Congress Cataloging in Publication Data
Leopardi, Giacomo, 1798–1837.
Pensieri.
Reprint. Originally published: Baton Rouge :
Louisiana State Univeristy Press, © 1981.
Includes bibliographical references.
I. Di Piero, W. S.   II. Title.
[PQ4708.P6E5 1984]   851'.7   84-14689
ISBN 0-19-503496-1 (pbk.)

Printing (last digit): 9 8 7 6 5 4 3 2 1

Printed in the United States of America

To my mother

CONTENTS

TRANSLATOR'S INTRODUCTION

To most American readers, the work of Giacomo Leopardi remains, more by oversight than by design, a still rather vague but glorious rumor. Many are familiar with the great lyrics—"A Silvia," "L'infinito," "La ginestra," and "A se stesso"—and with the brilliant imaginary dialogues of the *Operette morali*. But it must also be said that Leopardi impressed himself so deeply on European intellectual history of the past 150 years that Nietzsche, for example, could speak of him as "the greatest stylist of the century," ranking him alongside Goethe as one of the great poet-scholars. And that Leopardi's great obsessions still inspirit a good deal of modern Italian literature, whose major figures—Montale, Ungaretti, Svevo, Vittorini, Pavese—have in turn influenced recent American writing. It is only a slight exaggeration to say that Leopardi is everywhere present in the tradition of classical modernism.

Leopardi's place in early nineteenth-century letters is a rather peculiar one, and not simply because he was one of the great solitaries of the age. The early nineteenth century in Italy was a time of intellectual fervor, much of it due to the polemics emerging from the Romantic movement that had descended from France. Italian Romanticism did not lack strong and interesting voices. Tommaso Grossi, Melchiorre Cesarotti, Giovanni Berchet, and Silvio Pellico were all influential in shaping the intellectual tone of the age. For the most part, however, they remained yoked to the intellectual contingencies of the

1

period. Like Robert Southey and Thomas Love Peacock, they
were so claimed by contemporary cultural values that they remained neatly contained within the definitions of their time; to
later generations, their voices lack urgency and often seem
harmlessly archaic. Leopardi, on the other hand, was not contained by the conventional polemics of his time. Although
early in his career he participated briefly in the Romantic-
Classic controversy, taking for the most part the latter side, he
cannot be conveniently labeled a Romantic.[1] His ambitions
were certainly grander than those of any of his contemporaries. Like Blake, he seems one of those artists who spill out of
their own time and flood intellectual frontiers; and like Blake,
he risked extremism of the most provocative sort, probing and
testing the boundaries of consciousness rather than merely de-
lineating them. Although the work of some of his contemporaries still urges itself upon us—most notably Manzoni's *I pro-
messi sposi*, Foscolo's poetry and his prose book *The Last Letters*

1. Leopardi's essay, "Discorso di un italiano intorno alla poesia romantica,"
written in 1818 but not published till 1906, was a reply to several guidelines to
the composition of poetry laid down by Ludovico Di Breme in his "Osservazioni sulla poesia moderna." Di Breme argued that the new Romantic poetry
should draw its subject matter from contemporary customs and events; draw-
ing sharp lines between Classic and Romantic art, he said that while the ancients appeal to our imagination, the moderns should appeal instead to sentiment—immediacy of effect was to be prized over remoteness of dramatic
event. Leopardi answered that a poem's "modernity" is not defined by its subject, and he attacked the Romantic tendency to confuse originality and imaginative invention with mere novelty of subject or idea. He also speaks on
behalf of "sentiment" in Homer, noting however that Homer's appeal to sentiment is natural and un-self-conscious, whereas the sentiment espoused by the
Romantics is "pathetic"—that is to say, it has designs on the reader. To Leopardi, the true poet imitates nature naturally ("non imita veramente la natura
chi non la imita con naturalezza"); true poetry is therefore casual and spontaneous, not deliberate and affected. Giovanni Carsaniga has noted that Leopardi opposed Di Breme's theories "because they seemed to reduce the essence
of poetry to being 'pathetic' or sentimental; that is, not about the powerful un-
reflected natural images that excite human emotion, but about the emotions
themselves treated in a cold intellectual way." Giovanni Carsaniga, *Giacomo
Leopardi* (Edinburgh: University of Edinburgh Press, 1977), 23.

of Jacopo Ortis, and Pellico's *Le mie prigioni*—they are not comparable to the huge speculative intelligence and lyric gifts of Leopardi. And it is precisely this speculative intelligence that has remained inaccessible to American readers.

Leopardi's sensibility, his way of feeling and of thinking about feeling, dramatized the tragedy of values that was to become the central story of Western culture after 1848, that neurotic embrace of public self-esteem and private self-loathing rooted in the politics of social power. The influence of this sensibility crosshatches intellectual history. If Nietzsche was the most immediate and prominent heir to Leopardi's critical temperament, Leopardi's influence in our own time has been most evident in the writings of Cesare Pavese. The coincidences are eloquent. In 1938, Pavese confided to his diary: "Leopardi's 'illusions' are with us again." One of these illusions, many of which are anatomized in the *Pensieri*, regards the token altruism and generosity of others. In our dealings with the world, Leopardi says, we are always inclined to think that people will take pity on our misfortunes, perhaps even volunteer a helping hand. Charity is, after all, the first precept of Christian behavior. But Christian values have become for the most part a gross, though elegant, imposture: nothing in this world is freely given without something sooner or later being taken in exchange. At best, Leopardi suggests, charity is an instrument of self-esteem. "No one," Pavese writes in his diary, "absolutely no one, ever makes sacrifices without expecting something in return. It's all a matter of buying and selling."

In 1950, at the peak of fame and worldly success, Pavese committed suicide in a hotel room in Turin. In 1824, Leopardi analyzed what seemed to him our peculiarly modern style of suicide:

> What do all these voluntary deaths mean if not that men are tired and fiercely despairing of this existence? In ancient times men

killed themselves as a heroic gesture, or for grand illusions, or from violent passions etc. etc. and their deaths were illustrious etc. But now that heroism and grand visions have disappeared, and passions are so sapped of energy, why is it that the number of suicides is so much greater? And not just among great men who have failed in the grand manner, nourished on grand dreams, but men of all classes, so that even grand suicides are no longer "illustrious" . . . It means that our knowledge of things brings about this desire for death etc. Men now take their lives coldly.

(*Fragment on Suicide*)

These reflections on suicide also describe the dissolution of the conventional heroic personality that had long been another of Europe's most precious illusions. Here as elsewhere Leopardi called falsehood by its real name. If conventional heroism was no longer a medium for defining one's meaning, something else had to be taking its place. What Leopardi saw in the early years of his century was a civilization more and more preoccupied with its own unknowing, a world in which emptiness and forced inaction were so present as to seem a new, all-pervading substance. In this revised moral landscape, heroism for Leopardi became an interiorized condition that required, as Walter Benjamin later noted, "perseverance and insight, cunning and curiosity."[2] And one of the great forces against which the new hero had to test himself was *ennui*, or *noia*. Here, too, in his awareness of and struggle with *ennui*, Leopardi prefigured one of the most crucial concerns of subsequent poets and novelists.[3]

2. Walter Benjamin, *Critiche e recensioni* (Turin: Einaudi, 1979), 68.

3. "No two poets have anticipated more clearly the spirit of modern literature, have helped, through their works, in bringing it about and in strengthening, enriching, and interpreting it, more efficaciously and more unequivocally than Leopardi and Baudelaire; and in so far as Leopardi, in some ways, anticipated by a few years even Baudelaire himself, he may be considered to be the first to have done so." G. Singh, *Leopardi and the Theory of Poetry* (Kentucky: University of Kentucky Press, 1964), 258.

The more we know, Leopardi says, the more we want to die;
all learning is an education in mortality, all knowledge leads finally to a knowledge of annihilation. He was speaking from a
position of authority. He was one of the most learned men of
his day, his intellect and imagination as ample as Coleridge's,
his honesty as spacious and as devastating as Blake's. And we
know from his poems, letters, and daybooks that he enter-
tained the possibility of suicide—as his entire life was an exploration into Possibility—so we can be sure he was familiar with
its barbarous invitation.[4]

Throughout his brief and difficult life, however, Leopardi
opted time and again for energy and survival, often improvis-
ing his existence out of the contest between knowledge and
illusions:

> Illusions, however weakened and unmasked by reason, always
> stay with us and form the major part of our lives. Even if we
> know everything, this still isn't enough to dispel them, even if
> we know the illusions are vain. Nor, once lost, are they lost in
> such a way that their vital roots are also destroyed: if we go on
> living they are bound to flower again despite all our experience
> and certitude. . . . I've had the same thing happen to me hun-
> dreds of times, to despair completely because I was unable to
> die, then resume my old plans, building castles in the air regard-
> ing my future and even feeling a little passing cheerfulness.
>
> (*Zibaldone*, August 18–20, 1820)

Leopardi's life, as we shall see, was a constant dispute between
knowledge and illusion, and from this he fashioned his writings, the best of which are quarrels, dialogues with darkness,
teasing and inciting the possibilities of the human project.

4. "Leopardi poses the problem of suicide in terms very similar to those
that Camus was to employ in his more methodical examination of the same
question in *The Myth of Sisyphus*. According to Leopardi, victory could be
achieved over ennui only at the price of a redefinition of man's nature or at the
price of self-destruction." Reinhard Kuhn, *The Demon of Noontide* (Princeton:
Princeton University Press, 1976), 287.

Anyone who makes himself a student (and therefore a critic) of illusions and of human possibilities must be willing to follow wherever his explorations lead and willing to call things by their real names. Illusions must be made to yield to the power of one's will-to-speculate. In Leopardi, as later in Nietzsche, this will was absolute, and it was necessarily joined to great courage of mind and sentiment.[5] The results, as we might expect, are not at all genteel:

> Everything is evil. I mean, everything that is, is wicked; every existing thing is an evil; everything exists for a wicked end. Existence is a wickedness and is ordained for wickedness. Evil is the end, the final purpose, of the universe. Order, the state, laws, the natural process of the universe are all quite simply evil and are directed exclusively toward evil. The only good is nonbeing; the only really good thing is the thing that is *not*, things that are *not* things; all things are bad. All that exists, the totality of the many worlds that exist, the universe, are nothing but a minor blemish, a mote in metaphysics. Existence, in its general nature and essence, is an imperfection, an irregularity, a monstrosity. But this imperfection is a very small thing, truly just a blemish, because all existing worlds, however numerous or grand they may be, though not for certain infinite in number or size, are consequently infinitely small compared to what the universe *could* be, if it were infinite. And all that exists is infinitely small compared as it were to the true infinity of nonexistence, of nothingness.[6]   (*Zibaldone*, April 19, 1826)

5. "One must be honest in intellectual matters to the point of hardness . . . one must never ask whether the truth will be useful or whether it may become one's fatality. A preference of strength for questions for which nobody today has the courage; the courage for the forbidden." Quoted in Walter Kaufmann, *Nietzsche: Philosopher, Psychologist, Antichrist* (Rev. ed.; Princeton: Princeton University Press, 1974), 114. And while working on the third part of *Zarathustra*, Nietzsche wrote to his friend Gast that "Schopenhauer and Leopardi will seem like children and beginners beside his (Zarathustra's) pessimism."

6. The Italian here is worth quoting at length as an example of Leopardi's trim and vigorous language: "Tutto è male. Cioè tutto quello che è, è male; che ciascuna cosa esista è un male; ciascuna cosa esiste per un fin di male; l'esistenza è un male e ordinata al male; il fine dell'universo è il male; l'ordine e lo

Such writing, such thinking, is likely to make even the most tenacious reader cringe. Leopardi's absolutism is staggering, undistracted by wit (any suggestion of wit would seem rather pointless in this context). But we learn immediately thereafter that he poses all this as one more risky, unfashionable, unlikable possibility: "This system, though it offends our ideas, which hold that the end of all things can only be goodness, may perhaps be more tenable than Leibnitz's formulation, or Pope's, that 'everything is good.' I'm not anxious, however, to extend my system so far as to say that the existing universe is the worst of all possible universes, thus replacing optimism with pessimism. Who can ever know the limits of possibility?" It is in all events wrong, then, to dismiss Leopardi as merely an eloquent pessimist. I daresay that he, like Gramsci after him, would have thought pessimism at best a "vulgar mood." What most inspirited Leopardi was his desire for clarity and his need to explore possible truths.

Another thing that distinguishes Leopardi from his contemporaries is his clear and unrelenting perception of the self-reflective and self-revisionary nature of consciousness. He was able to describe, analyze, and transform into poetry the painful maneuvers of mind turning back upon itself. He possessed that special ability to observe himself observing and to feel

---

stato, le leggi, l'andamento naturale dell'universo non sono altro che male, nè diretti ad altro che al male. Non v'è altro bene che il non essere: non v'ha altro di buono che quel che non è; le cose che non son cose; tutte le cose sono cattive. Il tutto esistente; il complesso dei tanti mondi che esistono; l'universo; non è che un neo, un bruscolo in metafisica. L'esistenza, per sua natura ed essenza propria e generale, è un'imperfezione, un'irregolarità, una mostruosità. Ma questa imperfezione è una piccolissima cosa, un vero neo, perchè tutti i mondi che esistono, per quanti e quanto grandi che essi sieno, non essendo però certamente infiniti nè di numero nè di grandezza, sono per conseguenza infinitamente piccoli a paragone di ciò che l'universo potrebbe essere se fosse infinito; e il tutto esistente è infinitamente piccolo a paragone della infinità vera, per dir così, del non esistente, del nulla."

himself feeling. Leopardi and Foscolo shared a classical passion for lamentation and complaint, and their tone (rather than content) identifies them as near contemporaries. But Leopardi plunged more deeply into the complex mysteries of yearning, and his song is at times a psychology of morbid self-consciousness—it animates for us the condition of being conscious of consciousness. A morbidity, it must be remembered, that he always contested and hoped to defeat. With such a high theme—the dynamics of yearning frustrated so regularly by the barrenness or failure or paltriness of human possibility—Leopardi's work, the bulk of it, is tragic in mood and intent. The necessary sorrow of existence lies in the disjunction between the infinity of our desires and the frustrations imposed by human limits. We can see what we can never be.

Leopardi looked for a fixed center of the universe and found none. Unlike Manzoni, that other colossus of nineteenth-century Italy, Leopardi refused the consolations of Christian belief, refused to believe that nature is governed by Divine and ultimately benign Law. Nor did he swear allegiance to classical norms. Though he had a great but often mixed admiration for Greek culture, he did not enslave himself to the worship of things ancient; he was too familiar with the Greeks to be pious toward them. Leopardi's universe is recognizably modern, a blasted place, and nature is *il brutto poter*—brute force, mindless, governed by natural selection, empowered by its own necessities, oblivious to man's needs. In the *Zibaldone* he writes: "Nature, compelled by its law of destruction and reproduction, and in order to preserve the present state of the universe, is essentially, regularly, and perpetually the persecutor and mortal enemy of all individuals of every sort and species that Nature itself brings to birth. Nature begins to persecute them the very moment it gives birth to them." (April 11, 1829).

And in one of the *Operette morali*, "Dialogue Between Nature and an Icelander," the lonely mortal makes his case:

> I have to conclude, then, that you are the manifest enemy of mankind, of all other animals, and even of your own works. I realize now that we are doomed to suffer just as we are fated to be unhappy, and that it's as impossible to lead a peaceful life as it is to lead an active one without misery. You trap us, you threaten us, you sting us, you spite us, you tear us apart—always nothing but injury and persecution.

In such an inimical universe, man's life will tend more and more to become a struggle of brutalized resistance. Such resistance is one of the central subjects of the *Pensieri*.

In his autobiographical fragment, *Storia di un'anima*, Leopardi wrote with chilling brevity about his beginnings: "All I'll say about my origins is that I was born of a noble family in an ignoble town." Giacomo's father, Conte Monaldo Leopardi, was a kind and noble gentleman given to shaky business enterprises and very conservative politics. The Leopardi family at that time was one of the most important families of Recanati, a small city that sits on a low hill in the Marches some fifteen miles from the Adriatic coast. Monaldo was a self-styled man of quality, a strong personality with an abiding sense of self-importance. Social custom, which plays such an important part in the *Pensieri*, was the fixed standard against which Monaldo measured and judged all human behavior. In his later years he boasted of being the last man in Italy still to wear a sword, and in his memoirs he says that he always sought to dress "in a noble and decorous manner." Esteem—of himself, and that of others for him—was the gravitational center of Monaldo's life, and most of his activity converged on that still point where esteem is inflated by will. Again in his memoirs: "All that I have

ever come in contact with, has been done according to my will, and all that has not accorded with it seemed to me poorly done." In the *Pensieri*, Leopardi hardens this even more and says that the strong live in accordance with their own will, the weak in accordance with the will of others.

The strong-willed Monaldo married the Marchesa Adelaide Antici, the daughter of a Recanati nobleman. The marchesa, too, was a strong-willed individual, even more so than her husband; soon her authority in *casa Leopardi* eclipsed his, and she became the real governor of their household. She ran a frugal household, as a way of reconsolidating what was left of the Leopardi fortune after it had been drained by Monaldo's failed financial schemes. The marchesa's thrift was more than matched by her stern religiosity. She was in many ways a passionately self-sacrificial woman, fully devoted to the bizarre forms of Christian self-scourging then encouraged by the Church. Giacomo has described her as a woman who "was not in the least superstitious, but most orthodox and scrupulous in her Christian faith and practice." Pain, to Leopardi's mother, was a benison, and suffering a passport to salvation. Giacomo was convinced that his mother sincerely envied other mothers whose children died at birth, "for these children, escaping all perils, had flown directly to heaven." She thought beauty a great misfortune—the suffering that attends physical deformity was a gift from God. "Seeing her children ugly or deformed," wrote her son, the hunchback, "she gave thanks to God."

Giacomo, born June 29, 1798, was their first child. We are told that he was a healthy and spirited boy. In his childhood games with his beloved younger brother Carlo, Giacomo would always insist on playing the most heroic roles. He had a great love of fairy tales and ghost stories; like so many children, he was thrilled by his own terror. The lively child grew

up into a studious boy. By the age of twelve, having studied for years under private tutors, he already had more than a working knowledge of Latin and had mastered the fundamentals of theology, physics, and rhetoric. The first great movement in Leopardi's life came when Monaldo opened the doors of his library to the boy. Giacomo was then fourteen and ready to pursue his education on his own. His father's library, accumulated over many years, offered generous if at times eccentric resources for a young classical scholar. There were all the tools for learning languages—grammars, dictionaries, glossaries, textual commentaries—and the young student began to accumulate languages enthusiastically. There were texts in Hebrew, Greek, Latin, English, Spanish—the library would become Giacomo's refuge wherein he might teach himself the history of his race. He was fondest of philology and the classical authors, and his passion for learning seemed inexhaustible. These were the years of rigor in which he acquired what he called his "peregrine and recondite erudition." Between the ages of thirteen and seventeen, he began to write in earnest, producing a number of learned works—a history of astronomy, an essay entitled "On the Popular Errors of the Ancients," translations of Moschus, plays, verse, philosophical "dissertations," and other ambitious works. The adolescent would enter the library in the morning and study till late at night. When the evening sea-chill swept through *palazzo Leopardi*, he had to wrap himself in rugs to keep the cold out of his bones. Even as the flame twisted and guttered on the candle, Leopardi remained hunched over his small reading-desk in the library, hounded by the need to learn, a compulsion he himself did not fully understand. It was, in his own words, a period of "studio matto e disperatissimo," of mad and incredibly desperate study.

One day in his eighteenth year, Giacomo looked in a mirror

and saw himself *senza illusioni*. Though he always referred to himself as *un gobbo*, a hunchback, he wasn't quite. He suffered from scoliosis, a curvature of the spine that often occurs during childhood or adolescence. The years of intense study had twisted his body permanently, the scoliosis had raised a small double hump on his back and chest. The body remembers itself, and Giacomo surely recalled that as a child he had been straight-spined, noble in profile, upright in appearance rather than collapsed. His desire to know and to learn had created what he thought to be a physical monstrosity (*una mostruosità*, one of the key words in his vocabulary). Among men, he says in the *Pensieri*, appearances count for everything. At the age of twenty, he wrote to his friend and mentor Giordani:

> I have miserably and irremediably ruined myself by rendering my external appearances hateful and contemptible . . . [and] this is the only part of a man that most people take into account. Not just ordinary people, but even those who want virtue to have some physical adornment, when they find me utterly lacking such adornment they certainly will never love me—they won't dare love a man who possesses only beauty of soul.

Love and illusion. Most of Leopardi's life was suspended between these two terrible needs. Life nurtures itself on one or the other, or both combined. And both consume: "I consider love the most beautiful thing on earth, and find nourishment in illusion. . . . I don't think that illusions are totally vain, but rather that they are, to a certain degree, substantial and innate in all of us—and they form the whole of our life."

In his early manhood Leopardi began to languish in Recanati. Like any provincial place, it had little to offer an ambitious man of letters craving recognition. And to one as sensitive as Leopardi, the insular meanness of provincial gossip must have proved especially painful. At twenty-one, Leopardi

had never yet been away from Recanati; indeed, he had spent precious little time outside the walls of the family *palazzo*. He was still completely dependent on his father for financial support. The Leopardi household, once his monastic sanctuary, now began to seem a prison to the aspiring philologist-poet, and Giacomo's days there descended steadily into melancholy and self-pity. Moreover, although Monaldo was proud of his son's scholarship, he was not at all keen on the poetry that Leopardi was writing: at a time when the Austrians occupied large parts of northern Italy and had spies everywhere, the patriotic odes that Giacomo had been composing made his practice of poetry a pastime rather dangerous for the entire Leopardi household. But there was a deeper and more compelling reason for Leopardi's desire to break away from his family, a reason he describes in *pensiero* II: so long as he was dependent on his father, he could never be psychologically whole, he would remain forever an extension of his father's purse, a mere function of his father's will. Leaving *casa Leopardi* was not simply a question of pride, it was one of survival. Finally, in his twenty-fourth year, Giacomo was able to break—or at least stretch—the familial bonds and accompany one of his uncles to Rome.

Big-city life shocked the provincial youth. Rome turned out to be more than Leopardi had bargained for. Soon after his arrival there, he began to feel crushed and exasperated by the gross indifference of the city, a *noncuranza* felt all the more keenly by a young soul seeking fame and fortune. (Leopardi was to remain very sensitive to the problems and dilemmas experienced by young men entering society; much of what he says about this in the *Pensieri* is based on his personal experience.) Rome seemed outsized, monstrous, too monumental. Most people there, Leopardi felt, withdrew into indifference. He wrote to his brother Carlo:

Small-town life may be boring, but men there at least feel some
connection to one another and to the things around them, because the range and ambience of these relationships are modest,
limited, made on a human scale. But in a big city a man lives
without any relation whatsoever to the things around him; the
context is so vast that no individual can possibly fill it or even be
fully *aware* or it, and hence there's no point of contact among
them. You can imagine, then, how much greater—and how
much more terrible—the tedium of a great city must be than that
of a small town. Human indifference, which is a horrible feeling,
or rather an *absence* of feeling, must inevitably be concentrated in
big cities.

Rome was then, as it is now, a city where the social elite of the
age gathered. Physical deformity of any kind was bound to
elicit either disdain, embattled indifference, or snobbish pity.
Having finally managed to escape the loneliness of Recanati,
Leopardi now felt even lonelier and more wretched than before, and he began to yearn (almost despite himself) for those
familiar affections he had felt at Recanati.

He had gone to Rome hoping to dispel the solitude he
endured in Recanati. He was eager to experience a larger,
more comprehensive social environment. The *figlio di famiglia*
yearned for real human community, for the company of intelligent men and women (intelligent enough, he hoped, to appreciate *his* intelligence). But he felt that the architectural scale
of Rome conspired against human communication. It's worth
noting in some detail Leopardi's response, because it gives us
an early view of what would later become his own peculiar radical humanism. To the young poet, Rome's heroic spaces were,
in the end, antihuman: "Rome's colossal size serves no other
purpose than to multiply distances, multiply the number of
steps you must climb to find whomever you're looking for.
These huge buildings and interminable streets are just so many

spaces thrown between men, instead of being spaces that *contain* men." Later in his career, he broadened his argument on behalf of human proportions and the importance of the individual, insisting that the individual must not allow himself to be totally absorbed (and hence disintegrated) by any larger abstract unit, whether that unit be society, political party, state, or intellectual coterie. Like all radical humanists, Leopardi distrusted anything that hinted of mass identity and decimation of the individual self. In his time, he was perhaps closer in his radicalism to the aged Sartre than to his contemporary Mazzini. After a couple of failed attempts to gain employment in Rome, Leopardi returned to Recanati, this time hoping to find "nothing but friendship and love"—the two vital signs he had so profoundly missed in the capital.

Predictably, however, soon after his return home he felt again oppressed by his dependence on his father. Thus, when in 1825 he was offered a job by a Milanese publisher to work on an edition of Cicero, he immediately resolved to leave Recanati again. But he found Milan, then a center of political activism and Liberal opinion, quite as impersonal a place as Rome. Leopardi craved notice and esteem. He received very little of either. After a few months there, he traveled south to Bologna, which he had passed through on his journey to Milan. Here in *La Dotta*, a city of intellect that was also city-as-village, Leopardi felt very much at home. He was at ease on the gently curved streets of Bologna, where the porticoes neatly defined a self-contained, man-sized space and where the sidewalks seemed so perfectly adapted to personalized communication. Here was a place where an individual could partake of a larger community and feel himself a functional member of a city without being swamped by it. Leopardi was soon accepted into literary society and became rather famous for his poetry and

scholarship. His conversation was sought after. He found himself a success and was, for a time, happy.[7]

After spending brief periods in Florence and Pisa in 1826 and 1827, Leopardi returned to Recanati, having failed to obtain regular employment with which to support himself. Carlo, who had been the poet's chief source of solace and friendship, had by this time left *casa Leopardi*, so Giacomo now felt more alone than ever before. His solitude was made more bitter by the petty meanness he encountered whenever he left the *palazzo*. Walking the streets, he was heckled and tormented by boys, his deformity an easy target for ridicule. He felt himself pressed on all sides—by the pesty boys, by his father's subsidy, by his mother's possessiveness, and by his own grand aspirations. Even the challenge and consolation of his books were no longer readily available to him. For years he had suffered from ophthalmia, and now the disease made it almost impossible for him to read for any length of time. Now even his books conspired to cause him pain. He continued to write poems whenever he could and to plan long prose works, one of them a "system" of his philosophy. If he had any hope for salvation, it was the totally secular salvation of the clarity of his own mind. His urge to live became one with his need to clarify and to explore the processes of his wretched consciousness.

In 1830, Leopardi was invited to Florence, where a wealthy patron offered to support him in his work. Again he left Recanati, now for the last time. In Florence he met for the second time Antonio Ranieri, whom he had known briefly during his first stay in Florence and who became Leopardi's closest friend

7. About this time, in the *Zibaldone*, Leopardi offered a provisional definition of happiness: "Happiness is nothing more than contentment with one's own being and one's mode of being, satisfaction, perfect love of one's own condition, no matter what that condition may be, even if it's most despicable" (August 30, 1826, Bologna).

and protector during the remaining seven years of the poet's life. After three difficult years in Florence, where his already fragile health continued to deteriorate, Leopardi took his doctor's advice and moved with Ranieri to the balmier climate of Naples. In 1832, he closed his daybooks, the *Zibaldone*, which he had begun many years before. In his last years he composed three of the finest poems of the century, "A se stesso," "La ginestra," and "Il tramonto della luna." In 1836, he left Naples to escape the cholera epidemic that threatened the city (and which he alludes to in *pensiero* VII). He could, and did, escape the cholera, but not the deterioration of his body. He died on June 21, 1837.

Sometime in 1832 Leopardi began to prepare for publication a booklet of aphorisms and reflections that he did not live to see printed. In 1845, Ranieri published them under the title *CXI Pensieri*. Many of the *pensieri* were excavated by Leopardi from his *Zibaldone*, the series of daybooks he had kept from 1817 to 1832 (though he had not added much to it after 1829; see the Appendix for correspondences between these two works.) To appreciate the rather special (and specialized) shape and function of the *Pensieri*, one must have some idea of what the *Zibaldone* contains. Leopardi's first *Zibaldone* entry speaks of the beginnings of Italian literature and of the function of the Good and the True in art. For the next fifteen years, through 4,525 manuscript pages, he kept an almost daily record of his thoughts, observations, and feelings. The range of knowledge displayed in the *Zibaldone* (or *Miscellany*) is astonishing and at times wonderfully unpredictable: philological notes; etymologies; lengthy attempts to formulate a working aesthetic; reflections on society, authors (classical and modern), metaphysics, and morality; aphorisms on women, tobacco, liquor,

clothing, politics, public relations, biology, genetics, psychology, and a variety of other topics, including autobiographical reminiscences.

Leopardi's purpose in writing the *Pensieri* was to compose "a book of reflections on the characteristics of men and on their conduct in society." He wanted the *Pensieri* to be quite a different text from the *Zibaldone*, both in style and purpose. To realize this ambition, he chose to draw freely from materials he had already touched upon in the *Zibaldone*, but he did not limit himself to these raw materials. I emphasize that these were raw materials, for in order to make his text cogent—and the *Pensieri* is nothing if not compact, tight, coherent—he had to re-work, compress or enlarge, formalize and redistribute those materials he selected from the *Zibaldone* and which appear there in a more amorphous, leisurely, and expansive form. The *Zibaldone* is an epic account of Leopardi's sensibility, but the *Pensieri* is considerably more than just a chapbook of conclusions siphoned off from these vast explorations. One of Leopardi's recent popular biographers insists that we must first of all take into consideration the importance the poet placed on "clarity and propriety of expression, which in the *Pensieri* reached the highest level Leopardi ever touched upon in prose."[8] Most importantly, these one hundred and eleven "thoughts" all converge on one central subject: man's activity in groups. The *Pensieri* constitutes a manual for self-preservation in modern Western society. It tells us how society in general functions and what an individual must do if he is to survive the inevitable collision between his own willful individuality and the anonymous collective demands of society.[9]

8. Italo de Feo, *Leopardi: l'uomo e l'opera* (Milan: Mondadori, 1972), 540. De Feo also suggests that Leopardi took as a stylistic model not Pascal, as many critics have assumed, but Guicciardini, who had written a book of maxims not unlike the *Pensieri* in content and inspiration.

9. "With the perfection of society and the progress of civilization, the

Leopardi begins his case with a practical generalization. It's important that we assume what he assumes, "that the world is a league of scoundrels against men of generosity, of base men against men of good will," for all of Leopardi's subsequent observations are corollaries of this axiom. We may question the veracity of this premise, and we may question Leopardi's authority to make such a mighty generalization (he was, after all, a very solitary man), but once this premise is accepted, everything that follows takes on a most persuasive cogency. The *Pensieri*, then, must be read not so much as a random assortment of aphorisms hacked and carved from the rough quarry of the *Zibaldone*, but rather as a coherent narrative of ideas, a carefully organized, self-contained text in which each part is related to some other.

If the world stands opposed to all that is good, then all of man's activity in society becomes a game of combative one-upmanship whereby scoundrels conspire to dominate men of *virtù*—a modern vulgarized form of classical *arete*. The scoundrels, Leopardi says, are by far the majority; while the meek and the honest struggle to survive, the wicked strive to prevail. Since the latter are so obviously at the advantage, most men will side with wickedness in any encounter with the good; everyone wants to be on the winning side in a dispute, even if it's the side of meanness and deceit. Scoundrels moreover are excellent public-relations men; they know how to manipulate their public image—and that of others—in such a way as to win supporters for their cause, their chief instrument being deceit. They pretend to be strong and courageous—a mask for cowardice and vain arrogance—because they know that this instills fear in most ordinary men. Through fear they acquire power, knowing that common people mistake power for

masses profit but individuality suffers; it loses strength, value, perfection, and thus happiness" (*Zibaldone*, September 5, 1828).

strength, a Napoleonic conceit that still functions in Western politics. This is not, however, Leopardi's understanding of genuine strength. A truly strong man is one who does not concern himself with the machinery of fear and intimidation, for he feels no need of them. His strength is not founded on deceit and imposture. But, Leopardi says, it is almost impossible to win over the hearts and minds of people except through deceit. The strong man, in effect, is bound to suffer from bad public relations. Though he may be strong in substance, he lacks a strong public *image*; in a world where appearances count for everything, such a man is more likely to be thought a weakling. Men will sooner be won over by the glibness of bullies—for in glibness lies public power—than by the silent self-containment of the strong.

There are, however, certain social values that may function ambivalently in this apparently absolutist structure. Artifice, for example, has both a positive and negative value, depending on its application. Scoundrels depend heavily on artifice to gain their advantage. But artists may use artifice as a means of serving the true and the good; metaphor, an instrument of truth, is artifice. Moreover, a certain amount of artifice is essential for one to get along in human company. If a man wishes to make himself likable, he must pretend interest in the conversation of others; since such conversation is usually dull or boring, one can *only* pretend interest. When a man compromises in this way, does he falsify himself utterly? Does he join the league of base and petty men? Not necessarily, for such a man still possesses self-esteem; he is merely making a necessary compromise, without which he would surely find himself excluded from the human group. Likewise, if a man chooses to participate in groups—it is always a conscious choice, or at least should be—he must learn to accept the meritocracy (often spurious) upon which all social action is based. Leopardi does

insist, however, that if one wishes to remain true to oneself, one's distinction in society must be grounded in truth. He further distinguishes between two kinds of superiority: *hauteur*, which is always forced and artificial, and an instrument for power; and natural (or "classical") superiority, whereby one achieves one's aspirations in an honest way. The two types are easily recognized. The haughty man is arrogant and imposing, his will a kind of blunt instrument. The naturally superior man, however, tends to be withdrawn, simple in manner, humble, self-contained. Unfortunately, most often the bullies prevail, while the simple superior men become victims of envy and *ressentiment*. In several instances in the *Pensieri*, Leopardi reminds us that ordinary people frequently resent natural superiority, and they loathe genius. Their hold on self-esteem is so insecure, so embattled, that they feel threatened by the mere presence of a man of true strength, all the more when he seems indifferent to social power-rituals.

Another axiom of human behavior is that "the world speaks absolutely consistently in one way and acts absolutely consistently in another." To ignore hypocrisy is hypocritical; furthermore, such innocence invites disaster and eventual exclusion from the community. Can hypocrisy ever be eliminated? Possibly, Leopardi says, if we were to tell the truth, if we were to "call things by their real names," if we were to give more credence to substance than to artifice, then the gap between words and deeds would be closed. Then there would be no need for gamesmanship, and human communication would no longer be forced to rely on euphemism and circumlocution. This is certainly a noble (and still unrealized) project. Leopardi, always alert to dangers and as a philologist concerned with the actualization or falsification of language-in-action, admits that any man who tells the truth is likely to be hated and will probably be thought a simpleton. Society sooner tolerates evil-doers,

sooner admires confidence men, than it tolerates a man who names them. Even people who privately oppose a politician's policies, for example, will rush to shake his hand in public; such power seems almost a sacred charm. This, Leopardi says, demonstrates man's weakness; it does not, however, excuse his wickedness. Leopardi's extraordinary tolerance of normal human shortcomings and the compassion he feels for men's foibles derive from his own recognition of the importance of illusion. One of the most gentle (yet firm—Leopardi is *always* firm) passages in the *Pensieri* occurs in XXIX: "in everything he does man needs some illusion and glamour, since truth is always too flawed and impoverished. . . . He lives for the promise of something more, and better, than what the world can actually give. Even Nature is deceitful toward man: it makes life congenial and tolerable only through imagination and artifice." A little later, he notes that "men are miserable by necessity yet determined to think themselves miserable by accident."

Leopardi traces the hatred men feel toward one another back to the hatred of animals for their fellow creatures. Ultimately, Nature is the mother, the author, of all conflict—even the harmonies found in nature are sustained only at the cost of death and normalized dissolution. He further suggests that the law of natural selection applies also to men, where survival belongs to the wiliest and best adapted. Life in society, then, requires adaptation. Though a man be honest and forthright in all things, for example, he must still keep his affairs (especially his financial affairs) to himself, for his secrets will not be honored by others. When in public, a man must guard his natural weak spots, for these are the first to be noticed by others, and the first attacked. Above all, a man must preserve self-esteem, though watchful that it does not become so bloated as to suffocate him. This self-esteem, along with the internal strength described earlier, usually goes hand in hand with simplicity of

manners: if you are strong, be prepared to find your simplicity (like that of Stendhal's Fabrizio) interpreted as arrogance, with unpleasant consequences. At all events, strength is essential to self-preservation, since "the world never faults a man who refuses to yield."

In the *Zibaldone*, Leopardi makes his case for radical skepticism: "Human reason, if it is to make any progress whatsoever, can never divest itself of skepticism. It embodies truth. Reason cannot discover truth except by doubting and departs from truth whenever it judges with certainty. Doubt not only allows us to discover truth (in keeping with the Cartesian principle), but truth itself consists essentially of doubt. He who doubts, knows—knows as much as can be known" (September 8, 1821). In the *Pensieri*, he instructs his readers in the practical application of skepticism. In the world, we must assume that duplicity and double-talk surround us. Men seldom really mean what they say. Apparently sincere offers of assistance and support are usually "nothing more than sheer syllabic noise." The only fixed point on the constantly sliding scale of social values is one's own self-referential moral strength: "Man is unable here on earth to trust in anything but his own strength." All social behavior derives from, and serves, self-interest. Moreover, what one *seems to be* is always more crucial (and more profitable and more readily justifiable) than what one truly *is*. Before all else, a man of substance must realize that "the world does not care much about substance, and often absolutely refuses to tolerate it."

If society is a jungle or perilous savannah, then deference and obsequiousness can only undermine one's will to self-preservation. Given the slightest opening, men will crush their weaker fellows: "Esteem cannot be bought with deference." Better to hold one's ground at whatever cost than seek the esteem of others by degrading oneself. Too much deference is a

sign of low self-esteem, and men generally are quickest to attack those who lack self-respect.

Although the advice Leopardi offers in the *Pensieri* is obviously stern, it never descends into mere grumbling or into intellectual bullying. Its purpose is analytical. This tactical manual of social customs—Benjamin called it a "working oracle" that teaches "the art of discretion for rebels"—constitutes finally a profoundly critical document of modern social behavior and a sketch in miniature of the reversal in human values that has taken place between ancient and modern times. The ancients, Leopardi reminds us again and again, insisted that a man *be* good, whereas moderns demand that a man only seem good. The concept of the world-as-enemy-of-the-good dates back only as far as the beginning of the Christian era, he notes in *pensiero* LXXXIV. It marks the beginning of an epoch in which false appearances have become a social norm and lying an axiom of human behavior, something to help us make it through the day. Throughout his career, Leopardi was concerned with the steady decay of human community. The *Pensieri* is a brief investigation into the origins and effects of that disease. If this book lacks the sardonic grace of the *Operette morali* and the fragmentary exuberance of the *Zibaldone*, it nonetheless remains a most intense and insinuating book. In Leopardi's hands, the aphorism and extended reflection become surgical instruments for probing man's relationship to his society, making the *Pensieri* Leopardi's most practical prose work.

A number of people helped me at various stages of this translation. Rosa Maria Bosinelli read the first drafts of each *pensiero*, patiently clarifying and elaborating on many passages in the Italian; her discipline and encouragement were invaluable to me. My thanks also to J. J. Watts for his suggestions regard-

ing English phrasing. And to William Arrowsmith goes my gratitude for having shared with me some of his expertise; his criticisms were crucial in helping me give final shape to this translation. Deepest thanks of all to my wife, who read and criticized the manuscript and shared the chores in preparing the final typescript. Finally, I'm grateful to the Graduate Council of Louisiana State University for a summer stipend that allowed me to finish this book.

PENSIERI

I

Io ho lungamente ricusato di creder vere le cose che dirò qui sotto, perchè, oltre che la natura mia era troppo remota da esse, e che l'animo tende sempre a giudicare gli altri da se medesimo, la mia inclinazione non è stata mai d'odiare gli uomini, ma di amarli. In ultimo l'esperienza quasi violentemente me le ha persuase: e sono certo che quei lettori che si troveranno aver praticato cogli uomini molto e in diversi modi, confesseranno che quello ch'io sono per dire è vero; tutti gli altri lo terranno per esagerato, finchè l'esperienza, se mai avranno occasione di veramente fare esperienza della società umana, non lo ponga loro dinanzi agli occhi.

Dico che il mondo è una lega di birbanti contro gli uomini da bene, e di vili contro i generosi. Quando due o più birbanti si trovano insieme la prima volta, facilmente e come per segni si conoscono tra loro per quello che sono; e subito si accordano; o se i loro interessi non patiscono questo, certamente provano inclinazione l'uno per l'altro, e si hanno gran rispetto. Se un birbante ha contrattazioni e negozi con altri birbanti, spessissimo accade che si porta con lealtà e che non gl'inganna; se con genti onorate, è impossibile che non manchi loro di fede, e dovunque gli torna comodo, non cerchi di rovinarle; ancorchè sieno persone animose, e capaci di vendicarsi; perchè ha speranza, come quasi sempre gli riesce, di vincere colle sue frodi la loro bravura. Io ho veduto più volte uomini paurosissimi, trovandosi fra un birbante più pauroso di loro, e una persona da bene piena di coraggio, abbracciare per paura le parti del birbante: anzi questa cosa accade sempre che le genti ordinarie si tro-

I

For a long time I tried not to believe the things I shall be saying here, for aside from the fact that my own nature was quite detached from such things and that the heart always tends to judge others on its own terms, my inclination has always been to love rather than hate my fellow man. Personal experience, however, has almost violently convinced me of certain things. And I'm sure that those readers who have had occasion to associate frequently with other people will admit that what I'm about to say is true. Everyone else will consider it an exaggeration, until experience (if they ever really experience human society) forces them to face the truth.

I say that the world is a league of scoundrels against men of generosity, of base men against men of good will. When two scoundrels meet for the first time, they recognize each other immediately, as if by signs, and manage to get along. Or if their interests preclude this, they at least feel a definite attraction and great mutual respect for each other. When one scoundrel has business dealings with another, he usually acts fairly, without trying to cheat the other. When dealing with honest men, however, the scoundrel is sure to act dishonestly whenever it serves his interests, and he will try to destroy them even if they are courageous and able to avenge their loss. For the scoundrel hopes that his tricks will triumph over their courage, and his hopes are almost always realized. I have often seen the most timid men, when caught between an even more timid scoundrel and a brave, honest man, side with the scoundrel out of fear. This is bound to happen whenever ordinary people find

vano in occasioni simili: perchè le vie dell'uomo coraggioso e
da bene sono conosciute e semplici, quelle del ribaldo sono occulte e infinitamente varie. Ora, come ognuno sa, le cose ig-
note fanno più paura che le conosciute; e facilmente uno si
guarda dalle vendette dei generosi, dalle quali la stessa viltà e
la paura ti salvano; ma nessuna paura e nessuna viltà è bastante a scamparti dalle persecuzioni segrete, dalle insidie, nè
dai colpi anche palesi che ti vengono dai nemici vili. Generalmente nella vita quotidiana il vero coraggio è temuto pochissimo; anche perchè, essendo scompagnato da ogni impostura, è
privo di quell'apparato che rende le cose spaventevoli; e spesso
non gli è creduto; e i birbanti sono temuti anche come corag-
giosi, perchè, per virtù d'impostura, molte volte sono tenuti
tali.

Rari sono i birbanti poveri: perchè, lasciando tutto l'altro, se
un uomo da bene cade in povertà, nessuno lo soccorre, e molti
se ne rallegrano; ma se un ribaldo diventa povero, tutta la città
si solleva per aiutarlo. La ragione si può intendere di leggeri:
ed è che naturalmente noi siamo tocchi dalle sventure di chi ci è
compagno e consorte, perchè pare che sieno altrettante minac-
ce a noi stessi; e volentieri, potendo, vi apprestiamo rimedio,
perchè il trascurarle pare troppo chiaramente un acconsentire
dentro noi medesimi che, nell'occasione, il simile sia fatto a
noi. Ora i birbanti, che al mondo sono i più di numero, e i più
copiosi di facoltà, tengono ciascheduno gli altri birbanti, anche
non cogniti a se di veduta, per compagni e consorti loro, e nei
bisogni si sentono tenuti a soccorrerli per quella specie di lega,
come ho detto, che v'è tra essi. Ai quali pare uno scandalo che
un uomo conosciuto per birbante sia veduto nella miseria;
perchè questa dal mondo, che sempre in parole è onoratore
della virtù, facilmente in casi tali è chiamata gastigo, cosa che
ritorna in obbrobrio, e che può ritornare in danno, di tutti loro.
Però in tor via questo scandalo si adoperano tanto efficace-

themselves in such a situation, for the ways of a courageous and well-intentioned man are simple and open, whereas those of a scoundrel are mysterious and infinitely diverse—and we all know that the mysterious frightens us more than the familiar. We can easily deal with the vengeance of generous men; our own fear and cowardice rescue us. But no amount of fear or cowardice is enough to save us from the secret persecutions, intrigues, and open attacks made against us by cowardly enemies. Generally speaking, true courage isn't much feared in everyday life; lacking all false appearances, it lacks the machinery of imposture that makes things fearful, and so people refuse to believe it. Yet scoundrels are feared and thought courageous because their pose, their imposture, often passes for courage.

Scoundrels are seldom poor. No one ever helps an honest man fallen into poverty, and many even rejoice at his misfortune, but if a scoundrel falls on hard times the entire town rushes to his aid. The reason for this is clear: we are naturally moved by the misfortune of an acquaintance or colleague because such misfortune seems a constant threat to us as well. So we gladly offer assistance whenever we can; if not, we are tacitly inviting the same indifferent treatment should we ever find ourselves in such an unfortunate position. Now the scoundrels of the world—who outnumber everyone else and have greater means at their disposal—regard all other scoundrels, even those they don't know by sight, as their companions and colleagues. And they feel duty-bound to help them in times of need because of that league which, as I've said, exists among them. They think it scandalous for a known scoundrel to be seen in poverty; since the world always honors virtue in words, it's quick to call personal misery "chastisement," which brings disgrace to all scoundrels and may even hurt their cause. Therefore they strive to avoid such scandal so effectively

mente, che pochi esempi si vedono di ribaldi, salvo se non sono persone del tutto oscure, che caduti in mala fortuna, non racconcino le cose loro in qualche modo comportabile.

All'opposto i buoni e i magnanimi, come diversi dalla generalità, sono tenuti dalla medesima quasi creature d'altra specie, e conseguentemente non solo non avuti per consorti nè per compagni, ma stimati non partecipi dei diritti sociali, e, come sempre si vede, perseguitati tanto più o meno gravemente, quanto la bassezza d'animo e la malvagità del tempo e del popolo nei quali si abbattono a vivere, sono più o meno insigni; perchè come nei corpi degli animali la natura tende sempre a purgarsi di quegli umori e di quei principii che non si confanno con quelli onde propriamente si compongono essi corpi, così nelle aggregazioni di molti uomini la stessa natura porta che chiunque differisce grandemente dall'universale di quelli, massime se tale differenza è anche contrarietà, con ogni sforzo sia cercato distruggere o discacciare. Anche sogliono essere odiatissimi i buoni e i generosi perchè ordinariamente sono sinceri, e chiamano le cose coi loro nomi. Colpa non perdonata dal genere umano, il quale non odia mai tanto chi fa male, nè il male stesso, quanto chi lo nomina. In modo che più volte, mentre chi fa male ottiene ricchezze, onori e potenza, chi lo nomina è strascinato in sui patiboli; essendo gli uomini prontissimi a sofferire o dagli altri o dal cielo qualunque cosa, purchè in parole ne sieno salvi.

II

Scorri le vite degli uomini illustri, e se guarderai a quelli che sono tali, non per iscrivere, ma per fare, troverai a gran fatica pochissimi veramente grandi, ai quali non sia mancato il padre nella prima età. Lascio stare che, parlando di quelli che vivono di entrata, colui che ha il padre vivo, comunemente è un uomo

that any scoundrel down on his luck (provided he is not a complete unknown) will somehow find convenient means to mend his affairs.

On the contrary, good and magnanimous men, so unlike the general run of mankind, are practically thought to be creatures of another species, and consequently not only are they *not* taken as companions and colleagues, but they are not even thought worthy of sharing in social rights. And it's obvious that the degree of persecution they suffer corresponds to the degree of wickedness and spiritual debasement of the age and the people among whom they live. For just as nature always tends to purge animal bodies of humors and elements that are unsuited to the proper makeup of such bodies, so too does nature strive to destroy or expel from large bodies of men those members who differ greatly from the norm, especially when such nonconformity constitutes opposition. Furthermore, good and generous men are usually despised because they are naturally sincere, and because they call things by their real names—a crime mankind never pardons. Men do not so much hate an evil-doer, or evil itself, as they hate the man who calls evil by its real name. Thus an evil-doer often becomes rich, honored, and powerful, while the man who identifies evil is dragged off to the gallows. For men are willing to suffer almost anything from each other or from heaven itself, so long as *true words* do not touch them.

II

Skim through the lives of famous men. If you look at those who are famous more in deed than in word, after much searching you will find very few truly great men who had a father when they were young. To speak only of those living on private incomes, a man whose father is still alive usually has no

senza facoltà; e per conseguenza non può nulla nel mondo:
tanto più che nel tempo stesso è facoltoso in aspettativa, onde
non si dà pensiero di procacciarsi roba coll'opera propria; il che
potrebbe essere occasione a grandi fatti; caso non ordinario
però, poichè generalmente quelli che hanno fatto cose grandi,
sono stati o copiosi o certo abbastanza forniti de' beni della fortuna insino dal principio. Ma lasciando tutto questo, la potestà
paterna appresso tutte le nazioni che hanno leggi, porta seco
una specie di schiavitù de' figliuoli; che, per essere domestica,
è più stringente e più sensibile della civile; e che, comunque
possa essere temperata o dalle leggi stesse, o dai costumi pubblici, o dalle qualità particolari delle persone, un effetto dan-
nosissimo non manca mai di produrre: e questo è un sentimento che l'uomo, finchè ha il padre vivo, porta perpetuamen-
te nell'animo; confermatogli dall'opinione che visibilmente ed
inevitabilmente ha di lui la moltitudine. Dico un sentimento di
soggezione e di dependenza, e di non essere libero signore di
se medesimo, anzi di non essere, per dir così, una persona intera, ma una parte e un membro solamente, e di appartenere il
suo nome ad altrui più che a se. Il qual sentimento, più profondo in coloro che sarebbero più atti alle cose, perchè avendo
lo spirito più svegliato, sono più capaci di sentire, e più oculati
ad accorgersi della verità della propria condizione, è quasi impossibile che vada insieme, non dirò col fare, ma col disegnare
checchessia di grande. E passata in tal modo la gioventù,
l'uomo che in età di quaranta o di cinquant'anni sente per la
prima volta di essere nella potestà propria, è soverchio il dire
che non prova stimolo, e che, se ne provasse, non avrebbe più
impeto nè forze nè tempo sufficienti ad azioni grandi. Così anche in questa parte si verifica che nessun bene si può avere al
mondo, che non sia accompagnato da mali della stessa misura:
poichè l'utilità inestimabile del trovarsi innanzi nella giovanezza una guida esperta ed amorosa, quale non può essere alcuno

personal resources, consequently he can do nothing in the world. All the more so in that he is at the same time rich in prospect and hence gives no thought to acquiring things through his own work, which in itself might occasion great deeds. This is not the usual case, however, since those who have done great things have usually been very or fairly well supplied with fortune's blessings from the very beginning. But allowing for all this, the paternal authority found in all nations governed by law brings with it a kind of manchild slavery which, being domestic, is even more strict and more immediately felt than civil slavery. And however much tempered by law, public custom, or the individual characteristics of those involved, such bondage is sure to be destructive. It instills a feeling that will plague a man's heart as long as his father is alive and will be reinforced by the unspoken but inevitable opinion that most people have of him. A feeling, that is, of dependency and subjection whereby he is neither free master of himself nor even as it were a whole person, but rather just a fragment or member, his identity belonging more to others than to himself. This feeling runs deepest in those best suited to a life of action. Being more alert in spirit, they are more sensitive to—and more quick to perceive the truth of—their situation. And this feeling is incompatible not just with the performance of great deeds, but even with the conceiving of something grand. Having spent his life in such a way, a man who at the age of forty or fifty feels a sense of self-authority for the first time, obviously no longer feels stimulated. And even if he felt stimulated, he would no longer have the drive, the strength, or the time to perform great deeds. So in this regard, too, it holds true that every portion of good in the world is matched by at least an equal measure of sorrow. For the invaluable usefulness of finding early in one's youth a skillful and affectionate guide totally

così come il proprio padre, è compensata da una sorta di nullità
e della giovanezza e generalmente della vita.

III

La sapienza economica di questo secolo si può misurare dal
corso che hanno le edizioni che chiamano compatte, dove è
poco il consumo della carta, e infinito quello della vista. Seb-
bene in difesa del risparmio della carta nei libri, si può allegare
che l'usanza del secolo è che si stampi molto e che nulla si
legga. Alla quale usanza appartiene anche l'avere abbandonati
i caratteri tondi, che si adoperarono comunemente in Europa ai
secoli addietro, e sostituiti in loro vece i caratteri lunghi, ag-
giuntovi il lustro della carta; cose quanto belle a vederle, tanto e
più dannose agli occhi nella lettura; ma ben ragionevoli in
un tempo nel quale i libri si stampano per vedere e non per
leggere.

IV

Questo che segue, non è un pensiero, ma un racconto, ch'io
pongo qui per isvagamento del lettore. Un mio amico, anzi
compagno della mia vita, Antonio Ranieri, giovane che, se
vive, e se gli uomini non vengono a capo di rendere inutili i
doni ch'egli ha dalla natura, presto sarà significato abbastanza
dal solo nome, abitava meco nel 1831 in Firenze. Una sera di
state, passando per Via buia, trovò in sul canto, presso alla
piazza del Duomo, sotto una finestra terrena del palazzo che
ora è de' Riccardi, fermata molta gente, che diceva tutta spa-
ventata: ih, la fantasima! E guardando per la finestra nella
stanza, dove non era altro lume che quello che vi batteva dentro da una delle lanterne della città, vide egli stesso come
un'ombra di donna, che scagliava le braccia di qua e di là, e nel
resto immobile. Ma avendo pel capo altri pensieri, passò oltre,

unlike one's own father, is matched by a kind of emptiness of youth and of life in general.[1]

III

The economic wisdom of this century can be measured in terms of books published in so-called "compact" editions, where the consumption of paper is minimal and the consumption of eyesight infinite—though one may argue, I suppose, that we need to conserve paper, since custom demands that much be printed but nothing read. Also related to this is the elimination of the Roman type commonly used in Europe in past centuries, now replaced by cursive characters—and the paper is now slicker, glossier. The more beautiful such things are to see, the more damage done to the eyes when read, which is sensible enough in an age when books are printed to be seen, not read.

IV

The following is not a *pensiero* but a story, which I set down here for the reader's amusement. In 1831 I lived in Florence with my friend and soul-companion, Antonio Ranieri, a young man whose name—if he lives and if men don't ruin the gifts nature has given him—will soon be famous.[2] One summer evening, while walking down Via Buia, he saw on a corner up by the Piazza del Duomo a crowd of people gathered beneath the ground-floor window of what is now the Palazzo Riccardi. They were all terrified and were saying "Oh! Oh! The Phantom!" Looking up through the window into a room illuminated only by the light of a street lantern, Ranieri saw what looked like a woman's shadow tossing its arms around, while the rest of the figure remained still. Being preoccupied with other

e per quella sera nè per tutto il giorno vegnente non si ricordò di quell'incontro. L'altra sera, alla stessa ora, abbattendosi a ripassare dallo stesso luogo, vi trovò raccolta più moltitudine che la sera innanzi, e udì che ripetevano collo stesso terrore: ih, la fantasima! E riguardando per entro la finestra, rivide quella stessa ombra, che pure, senza fare altro moto, scoteva le braccia. Era la finestra non molto più alta da terra che una statura d'uomo, e uno tra la moltitudine che pareva un birro, disse: s'i' avessi qualcuno che mi sostenessi 'n sulle spalle, i' vi monterei, per guardare che v'è là drento. Al che soggiunse il Ranieri: se voi mi sostenete, monterò io. E dettogli da quello, montate, montò su, ponendogli i piedi in sugli omeri, e trovò presso all'inferriata della finestra, disteso in sulla spalliera di una seggiola un grembiale nero, che agitato dal vento, faceva quell'apparenza di braccia che si scagliassero; e sopra la seggiola, appoggiata alla medesima spalliera, una rocca da filare, che pareva il capo dell'ombra: la quale rocca il Ranieri presa in mano, mostrò al popolo adunato, che con molto riso si disperse.

A che questa storiella? Per ricreazione, come ho detto, de' lettori, e inoltre per un sospetto ch'io ho, che ancora possa essere non inutile alla critica storica ed alla filosofia sapere che nel secolo decimonono, nel bel mezzo di Firenze, che è la città più culta d'Italia, e dove il popolo in particolare è più intendente e più civile, si veggono fantasmi, che sono creduti spiriti, e sono rocche da filare. E gli stranieri si tengano qui di sorridere, come fanno volentieri delle cose nostre: perchè troppo è noto che nessuna delle tre grandi nazioni che, come dicono i giornali, marchent à la tête de la civilisation, crede agli spiriti meno dell'italiana.

thoughts, however, he went on his way and for the rest of that evening and the following day he hardly remembered the incident. The following evening at the same time, he happened to pass by the same spot, where he found a crowd even larger than that of the evening before. And again he heard the people, still terrified, crying out repeatedly, "Oh! Oh! The Phantom!" Looking up through the window, he saw the same motionless shadow flailing its arms. The window was not much higher from the ground than a man's height, so someone in the crowd, a policeman apparently, said: "If someone wants to hold me, I'll climb up and have a look at what's inside." To this suggestion Ranieri replied: "I'll climb up, if you think you can hold me." So Ranieri boosted himself, his feet set squarely on the policeman's shoulders. Looking inside the room, he saw a black smock stretched out on the back of a chair close by the window-grating. When stirred by the wind, the smock gave the impression of flailing arms, and leaning against the rear side of the chair was a tall distaff, which created the illusion of the shadow's head. Taking the distaff in hand, Ranieri showed it to the people assembled below, who then dispersed laughing.

Why this little story? As I said, for the reader's entertainment. But also because I suspect that philosophy and historical criticism might learn something from it. Namely that in the nineteenth century, in the very heart of Florence, which is the most learned city in Italy and whose inhabitants are particularly discerning and sophisticated, people still see ghosts that they believe to be spirits—ghosts that are distaffs. Foreigners had better not laugh at this, as they do so willingly at our Italian ways, for it is too well known that of the three great nations which, as the journals say, *marchent à la tête de la civilisation*, Italy is the one least inclined to believe in ghosts.

V

Nelle cose occulte vede meglio sempre il minor numero, nelle palesi il maggiore. È assurdo l'addurre quello che chiamano consenso delle genti nelle quistioni metafisiche: del qual consenso non si fa nessuna stima nelle cose fisiche, e sottoposte ai sensi; come per esempio nella quistione del movimento della terra, e in mille altre. Ed all'incontro è temerario, pericoloso, ed al lungo andare, inutile, il contrastare all'opinione del maggior numero nelle materie civili.

VI

La morte non è male: perchè libera l'uomo da tutti i mali, e insieme coi beni gli toglie i desiderii. La vecchiezza è male sommo: perchè priva l'uomo di tutti i piaceri, lasciandogliene gli appetiti; e porta seco tutti i dolori. Nondimeno gli uomini temono la morte, e desiderano la vecchiezza.

VII

Havvi, cosa strana a dirsi, un disprezzo della morte e un coraggio più abbietto e più disprezzabile che la paura: ed è quello de' negozianti ed altri uomini dediti a far danari, che spessissime volte, per guadagni anche minimi, e per sordidi risparmi, ostinatamente ricusano cautele e provvidenze necessarie alla loro conservazione, e si mettono a pericoli estremi, dove non di rado, eroi vili, periscono con morte vituperata. Di quest'obbrobrioso coraggio si sono veduti esempi insigni, non senza seguirne danni e stragi de' popoli innocenti, nell'occasione della peste, chiamata più volentieri cholera morbus, che ha flagellata la specie umana in questi ultimi anni.

V

Mysterious things are always best perceived by the few, and obvious things by the many. It is absurd to cite what we call "a general consensus" on metaphysical questions; yet no one bothers with such consensus on physical things accessible to the senses, such as the movement of the earth and hundreds of other things. On the other hand, it is foolhardy, dangerous, and in the long run useless to stand opposed to majority opinion in civil matters.

VI

Death is not evil, for it frees man from all ills and takes away his desires along with desire's rewards. Old age is the supreme evil, for it deprives man of all pleasures while allowing his appetites to remain, and it brings with it every possible sorrow. Yet men fear death and desire old age.

VII

Strange as it may sound, I used to be disdainful of death, and I possessed a kind of courage even more base and contemptible than fear itself, the kind one finds among merchants and other men dedicated to making money. These craven heroes, in order to turn a profit or save a few pennies, almost always disregard the precautions necessary for self-preservation; they risk their lives and often die an ignominious death, and their adventures usually bring widespread death and destruction to innocent people. We have seen many blatant examples of this kind of shameful bravado during the outbreak of plague—more conveniently called *cholera morbus*—which has scourged mankind these recent years.[3]

VIII

Uno degli errori gravi nei quali gli uomini incorrono giornal-
mente, è di credere che sia tenuto loro il segreto. Nè solo il segreto di ciò che essi rivelano in confidenza, ma anche di ciò che
senza loro volontà, o mal grado loro, è veduto o altrimenti
saputo da chicchessia, e che ad essi converrebbe che fosse tenuto occulto. Ora io dico che tu erri ogni volta che sapendo che
una cosa tua è nota ad altri che a te stesso, non tieni già per
fermo che ella sia nota al pubblico, qualunque danno o vergogna possa venire a te di questo. A gran fatica per la considerazione dell'interesse proprio, si tengono gli uomini di non
manifestare le cose occulte; ma in causa d'altri, nessuno tace: e
se vuoi certificarti di questo, esamina te stesso, e vedi quante
volte o dispiacere o danno o vergogna che ne venga ad altri, ti
ritengono di non palesare cosa che tu sappi; di non palesarla,
dico, se non a molti, almeno a questo o a quell'amico, che torna
il medesimo. Nello stato sociale nessun bisogno è più grande
che quello di chiacchierare, mezzo principalissimo di passare il
tempo, ch'è una delle prime necessità della vita. E nessuna materia di chiacchiere è più rara che una che svegli la curiosità e
scacci la noia: il che fanno le cose nascoste e nuove. Però prendi
fermamente questa regola: le cose che tu non vuoi che si sappia
che tu abbi fatte, non solo non le ridire, ma non le fare. E quelle
che non puoi fare che non sieno, o che non sieno state, abbi per
certo che si sanno, quando bene tu non te ne avvegga.

IX

Chi contro all'opinione d'altri ha predetto il successo di una
cosa nel modo che poi segue, non si pensi che i suoi contraddit-
tori, veduto il fatto, gli dieno ragione, e lo chiamino più savio o

VIII

One of the serious everyday errors men commit is to believe their secrets are safe with others. Not just personal secrets disclosed in confidence, but also those bits of information, best left unspoken, which without our consent or against our wishes become public knowledge. If you know that some secret of yours is shared, for whatever reason, by one or two people, you would be wrong not to assume that your secret is known to everyone, however much this admission offends or embarrasses you. In the interest of self-protection, men are careful not to disclose their own secrets. But when it comes to other people, no man stays silent. For proof of this, simply examine yourself: consider how often (or how seldom) you hesitate to reveal something because you know it will displease, harm, or shame someone else. I don't mean reveal it to a large number of people but merely to this or that friend—it amounts to the same thing. In society, no need is greater than the need to make small talk. It's the most common way of passing time and is one of life's chief needs. And no subject of gossip is more precious than one that incites curiosity and dispels boredom, which is what spilled secrets do. So, stick to this rule: if you don't want people to know about certain things you've done, don't just refrain from talking about them, but rather *do not do them*. And as for things you cannot or could not help doing, rest assured that they are already known, even though you may not be aware of it.

IX

Say that a man, going against the opinion of others, has predicted something that later comes true in some way. Don't think that his contradictors will admit he is right, even after it's

più intendente di loro: perchè o negheranno il fatto, o la pre-
dizione, o allegheranno che questa e quello differiscano nelle
circostanze, o in qualunque modo troveranno cause per le quali
si sforzeranno di persuadere a se stessi e agli altri che l'opinione loro fu retta, e la contraria torta.

X

La maggior parte delle persone che deputiamo a educare i
figliuoli, sappiamo di certo non essere state educate. Nè du-
bitiamo che non possano dare quello che non hanno ricevuto, e
che per altra via non si acquista.

XI

V'è qualche secolo che, per tacere del resto, nelle arti e nelle
discipline presume di rifar tutto, perchè nulla sa fare.

XII

Colui che con fatiche e con patimenti, o anche solo dopo
molto aspettare, ha conseguito un bene, se vede altri conseguire il medesimo con facilità e presto, in fatti non perde
nulla di ciò che possiede, e nondimeno tal cosa è naturalmente
odiosissima, perchè nell'immaginativa il bene ottenuto scema a
dismisura se diventa comune a chi per ottenerlo ha speso e
penato poco o nulla. Perciò l'operaio della parabola evangelica
si duole come d'ingiuria fatta a se, della mercede uguale alla
sua, data a quelli che avevano lavorato meno; e i frati di certi
ordini hanno per usanza di trattare con ogni sorte di acerbità i

been proved, or that they will consider him wiser and more discerning than themselves. For either they will deny his prediction or the event, or else allege that something or other is inconsistent. Or they will find reasons to convince themselves and others that their own opinion was originally correct, and the contrary opinion wrong.

X

We can be sure that most of the people we appoint to educate our children have not been educated. Yet we assume that they can give something that they themselves have not received, and that this is the only way one can get an education.

XI

Some centuries presume to remake everything in the arts and other disciplines because they themselves do not know how to make anything.

XII

If a person has worked or suffered or waited a long time to obtain some advantage in life, it's no loss to him to see others obtaining the same advantage quickly and easily. And yet such a thing is by nature absolutely hateful to him. For he imagines that his hard-won advantage is diminished when shared by others who have suffered and expended little or nothing in acquiring it. Thus the laborer in the Gospel parable suffers a kind of personal insult when those who have worked less than he are paid the same wages.[4] And monks of certain religious orders customarily treat novices cruelly, afraid that they might

novizi, per timore che non giungano agiatamente a quello stato
al quale essi sono giunti con disagio.

XIII

Bella ed amabile illusione è quella per la quale i dì anniversari di un avvenimento, che per verità non ha a fare con essi
più che con qualunque altro dì dell'anno, paiono avere con
quello un'attinenza particolare, e che quasi un'ombra del passato risorga e ritorni sempre in quei giorni, e ci sia davanti:
onde è medicato in parte il tristo pensiero dell'annullamento di
ciò che fu, e sollevato il dolore di molte perdite, parendo che
quelle ricorrenze facciano che ciò che è passato, e che più non
torna, non sia spento nè perduto del tutto. Come trovandoci in
luoghi dove sieno accadute cose o per se stesse o verso di noi
memorabili, e dicendo, qui avvenne questo, e qui questo, ci
reputiamo, per modo di dire, più vicini a quegli avvenimenti,
che quando ci troviamo altrove; così quando diciamo, oggi è
l'anno, o tanti anni, accadde la tal cosa, ovvero la tale, questa ci
pare, per dir così, più presente, o meno passata, che negli altri
giorni. E tale immaginazione è sì radicata nell'uomo, che a
fatica pare che si possa credere che l'anniversario sia così alieno
dalla cosa come ogni altro dì: onde il celebrare annualmente le
ricordanze importanti, sì religiose come civili, sì pubbliche
come private, i dì natalizi e quelli delle morti delle persone
care, ed altri simili, fu comune, ed è, a tutte le nazioni che
hanno, ovvero ebbero, ricordanze e calendario. Ed ho notato,
interrogando in tal proposito parecchi, che gli uomini sensibili,
ed usati alla solitudine, o a conversare internamente, sogliono
essere studiosissimi degli anniversari, e vivere, per dir così, di
rimembranze di tal genere, sempre riandando, e dicendo fra
se: in un giorno dell'anno come il presente mi accadde questa o
questa cosa.

advance in the order without having suffered the same degree of hardship.

XIII

Another lovely and congenial illusion is the one by which anniversaries seem to have some special connection to the event they commemorate, when in fact the event has nothing more to do with these special days than with any other day of the year. Some faint shadow of the past seems to reappear and stand before us: it soothes our pained awareness of the disappearance of *what once was* and softens the sorrows of loss. For anniversaries make it seem that those things now gone forever are neither forgotten nor entirely lost. Whenever we find ourselves in places where certain things happened—things memorable in themselves or in their relation to us—we say, "*This is where it all happened.*" And we feel, as it were, closer to the actual event than we would elsewhere. Likewise, when we say, "*A year ago today, or many years ago today, such and such a thing happened,*" the event seems more present, or less past, than on other days. This fancy is so deeply rooted in man's imagination that it's hard for him to believe that an anniversary is just as remote from the actual event as any other day is. Thus the annual celebration of important memories—whether religious or civil, public or private, birthdays or requiems—was and is still common to all nations that have ever had calendars or memorials. In questioning a number of people on this, I've noticed that men of sensibility, those accustomed to solitude and self-reflection, are usually obsessed with anniversaries. They live, so to speak, on memories of this kind, always recollecting the past, always telling themselves: "*On a certain day of the year like today, such and such happened to me.*"

XIV

Non sarebbe piccola infelicità degli educatori, e sopratutto dei parenti, se pensassero, quello che è verissimo, che i loro figliuoli, qualunque indole abbiano sortita, e qualunque fatica, diligenza e spesa si ponga in educarli, coll'uso poi del mondo, quasi indubitabilmente, se la morte non li previene, diventeranno malvagi. Forse questa risposta sarebbe più valida e più ragionevole di quella di Talete, che dimandato da Solone perchè non si ammogliasse, rispose mostrando le inquietudini dei genitori per gl'infortunii e i pericoli de' figliuoli. Sarebbe, dico, più valido e più ragionevole lo scusarsi dicendo di non volere aumentare il numero dei malvagi.

XV

Chilone, annoverato fra i sette sapienti della Grecia, ordinava che l'uomo forte di corpo, fosse dolce di modi, a fine, diceva, d'ispirare agli altri più riverenza che timore. Non è mai soverchia l'affabilità, la soavità de' modi, e quasi l'umiltà in quelli che di bellezza, o d'ingengo o d'altra cosa molto desiderata nel mondo, sono manifestamente superiori alla generalità: perchè troppo grave è la colpa della quale hanno a impetrar perdono, e troppo fiero e difficile è il nemico che hanno a placare; l'una la superiorità, l'altro l'invidia. La quale credevano gli antichi, quando si trovavano in grandezze e in prosperità, che convenisse placare negli stessi Dèi, espiando con umiliazioni, con offerte e con penitenze volontarie il peccato appena espiabile della felicità o dell'eccellenza.

XIV

Educators, and certainly parents, would feel less than happy if they dared consider this indisputable truth: that their children, regardless of the temperament given them by nature, and despite the toil, diligence, and expense involved in educating them, will almost certainly turn wicked once they have experienced the ways of the world, provided death does not intervene. This answer may be more valid, and more reasonable, than that of Thales. When Solon asked him why he refused to take a wife, Thales replied by pointing out the extreme anxieties felt by parents over the dangers and misfortunes of their children.[5] It would, I think, be more valid and reasonable to excuse themselves by saying that it had never been their intention to increase the number of scoundrels.

XV

Chilon, esteemed one of the seven sages of ancient Greece, said that a man strong in body should also be gentle in manner; thus, Chilon said, he will inspire in others respect rather than fear.[6] Those who are obviously superior to most others in beauty, genius, or any of the other things so prized in our age, can never be *too* affable, gentle, or humble in their behavior. The sin for which they must ask forgiveness is too serious, the enemy they must placate too fierce and contentious: their sin is superiority, their enemy is envy. When the ancients were great and prosperous, they saw fit to appease even the envy of the gods. Their offerings, voluntary penances, and acts of self-mortification were ways of atoning for that hardly expiable sin of happiness, or excellence.

XVI

Se al colpevole e all'innocente, dice Ottone imperatore appresso Tacito, è apparecchiata una stessa fine, è più da uomo il
perire meritamente. Poco diversi pensieri credo che sieno quelli di alcuni, che avendo animo grande e nato alla virtù, entrati
nel mondo, e provata l'ingratitudine, l'ingiustizia, e l'infame
accanimento degli uomini contro i loro simili, e più contro i vir-
tuosi, abbracciano la malvagità; non per corruttela, nè tirati
dall'esempio, come i deboli; nè anche per interesse, nè per
troppo desiderio dei vili e frivoli beni umani; nè finalmente
per isperanza di salvarsi incontro alla malvagità generale; ma
per un'elezione libera, e per vendicarsi degli uomini, e rendere
loro il cambio, impugnando contro di essi le loro armi. La malvagità delle quali persone è tanto più profonda, quanto nasce
da esperienza della virtù; e tanto più formidabile, quanto è
congiunta, cosa non ordinaria, a grandezza e fortezza d'animo,
ed è una sorte d'eroismo.

XVII

Come le prigioni e le galee sono piene di genti, al dir loro,
innocentissime, così gli uffizi pubblici e le dignità d'ogni sorte
non sono tenute se non da persone chiamate e costrette a ciò
loro mal grado. È quasi impossibile trovare alcuno che confessi
di avere o meritato pene che soffra, o cercato nè desiderato
onori che goda: ma forse meno possibile questo, che quello.

XVI

If the same end awaits both the innocent and the guilty, says the Emperor Otho in Tacitus, then it is more manly to die for a good cause.[7] I believe that thoughts of this sort preoccupy certain men who, though of noble mind and born to virtue, will eventually turn wicked once they enter public life. For they will have experienced the ingratitude, injustice, and miserable hatred men show toward their own kind, most of all toward the virtuous. They turn wicked not from depravity, not from the weak man's emulation of others, not from self-interest or excessive desire for mean and frivolous profit, nor finally from any impulse to remain free of the general moral disease. Rather, they turn wicked by free choice, to avenge themselves, taking up arms against mankind and exacting measure for measure. The wickedness of such people is all the more profound when it results from their experience with virtue, all the more formidable when joined, however rarely, with strength and greatness of spirit—and it becomes a kind of heroism.

XVII

Just as prisons and galleys are filled with people who by their own account are absolutely innocent, so public offices and distinguished positions of every sort are occupied by people who allow themselves, unwillingly of course, to be appointed and forced into such positions. It is nearly impossible to find someone who admits either to deserving his punishment or to seeking or wanting the honors he now enjoys. But the latter, I think, is much less common than the former.

XVIII

Io vidi in Firenze uno che strascinando, a modo di bestia da tiro, come colà è stile, un carro colmo di robe, andava con grandissima alterigia gridando e comandando alle persone di dar luogo; e mi parve figura di molti che vanno pieni di orgoglio, insultando agli altri, per ragioni non dissimili da quella che causava l'alterigia in colui, cioè tirare un carro.

XIX

V'ha alcuna poche persone al mondo, condannate a riuscir male cogli uomini in ogni cosa, a cagione che, non per inesperienza nè per poca cognizione della vita sociale, ma per una loro natura immutabile, non sanno lasciare una certa semplicità di modi, privi di quelle apparenze e di non so che mentito ed artifiziato, che tutti gli altri, anche senza punto avvedersene, ed anche gli sciocchi, usano ed hanno sempre nei modi loro, e che è in loro e ad essi medesimi malagevolissimo a distinguere dal naturale. Quelli ch'io dico, essendo visibilmente diversi dagli altri, come riputati inabili alle cose del mondo, sono vilipesi e trattati male anco dagl'inferiori, e poco ascoltati o ubbiditi dai dipendenti: perchè tutti si tengono da più di loro, e li mirano con alterigia. Ognuno che ha a fare con essi, tenta d'ingannarli e di danneggiarli a profitto proprio più che non farebbe con altri, credendo la cosa più facile, e poterlo fare impunemente: onde da tutte le parti è mancato loro di fede, e usate soverchierie, e conteso il giusto e il dovuto. In qualunque concorrenza sono superati, anche da molto inferiori a loro, non solo d'ingegno o d'altre qualità intrinseche, ma di quelle che il mondo conosce ed apprezza maggiormente, come bellezza,

XVIII

Once in Florence I saw a man swaggering proudly down the street while dragging behind him, like some draft animal, a cart piled high with all sorts of stuff (a familiar sight there), shouting and ordering people to get out of his way. This seems to me an image of so many proud and swaggering men who act offensively toward others for reasons not unlike the one which inspired such arrogance in that Florentine—that is, they are pulling a cart.

XIX

There are some few people in the world doomed to fail in all their dealings with men because they do not know how to give up a certain simplicity of manner. Not because they are inexperienced or unfamiliar with social life, but rather because their nature is fixed, unchanging. They lack those appearances—those various kinds of falsehood and artifice—that all other men, simpletons included, have and use, often unawares, so that it becomes nearly impossible for them to distinguish the artificial from the natural. The few I speak of here, being noticeably different from others and thought incompetent in worldly matters, are vilified and mistreated even by their inferiors. Lesser men hardly ever obey or listen to them; all hold themselves superior to them and treat them with proud contempt. Each person who deals with such men tries to deceive them and to turn their harm to his own advantage, much more than he would with others, since he feels he can do so easily and with impunity. So that wherever they turn, they meet with broken promises, relentless oppression, and contested dues and rights. In competition of whatever sort, they are surpassed by men far inferior to themselves—inferior not

gioventù, forza, coraggio, ed anche ricchezza. Finalmente qualunque sia il loro stato nella società, non possono ottenere quel
grado di considerazione che ottengono gli erbaiuoli e i facchini.
Ed è ragione in qualche modo; perchè non è piccolo difetto o
svantaggio di natura, non potere apprendere quello che anche
gli stolidi apprendono facilissimamente, cioè quell'arte che sola
fa parere uomini gli uomini ed i fanciulli: non potere, dico, non
ostante ogni sforzo. Poichè questi tali, quantunque di natura
inclinati al bene, pure conoscendo la vita e gli uomini meglio di
molti altri, non sono punto, come talora paiono, più buoni di
quello che sia lecito essere senza meritare l'obbrobrio di questo
titolo; e sono privi delle maniere del mondo non per bontà, o
per elezione propria, ma perchè ogni loro desiderio e studio
d'apprenderle ritorna vano. Sicchè ad essi non resta altro, se
non adattare l'animo alla loro sorte, e guardarsi sopratutto di
non voler nascondere o dissimulare quella schiettezza e quel
fare naturale che è loro proprio: perchè mai non riescono così
male, nè così ridicoli, come quando affettano l'affettazione ordinaria degli altri.

XX

Se avessi l'ingegno del Cervantes, io farei un libro per pur-
gare, come egli la Spagna dall'imitazione de' cavalieri erranti,
così io l'Italia, anzi il mondo incivilito, da un vizio che, avendo
rispetto alla mansuetudine dei costumi presenti, e forse anche
in ogni altro modo, non è meno crudele nè meno barbaro di
qualunque avanzo della ferocia de' tempi medii castigato dal
Cervantes. Parlo del vizio di leggere o di recitare ad altri i componimenti propri: il quale, essendo antichissimo, pure nei secoli addietro fu una miseria tollerabile, perchè rara; ma oggi,
che il comporre è di tutti, e che la cosa più difficile è trovare

only in intelligence and other innate qualities, but even in
those the world recognizes and values, such as youth, beauty,
strength, courage, and even wealth. Finally, no matter what
their position in society, they fail to obtain the measure of respect accorded peddlers and porters. And in some ways this is
just, for it's no mean shortcoming or defect in a man's nature to
be incapable of learning something that comes easily even to
dunces, namely the one art that allows men and children to
seem human. Incapable, that is, despite every effort. For even
if naturally inclined toward goodness, knowing more about life
and mankind than most, they will try not to seem *too* good
(though they often appear so), since they know this carries a
certain stigma. They lack worldly manners not because of their
goodness, or by conscious choice, but rather because all their
hopes and efforts to acquire them are frustrated. Hence the
best they can do is try to accommodate their fate, and above all
try not to conceal or dissemble that purity and natural manner
which are their very own. For they never fail so miserably,
never seem so ridiculous, as when they affect the commonplace affectations of others.

XX

If I had Cervantes' genius, just as he purged Spain of the im-
itation of knights errant, I too would write a book purging
Italy—indeed, the entire civilized world—of a certain vice, one
which, with all due respect to the tameness of present customs, and perhaps in every other respect, is no less coarse and
barbaric than any remnant of medieval savagery chastised by
Cervantes. I mean the habit of reading or reciting one's own
compositions to others. This very ancient custom was in past
centuries a tolerable misery, since it was rare. But today, when
everybody can write and when the hardest thing to find is

uno che non sia autore, è divenuto un flagello, una calamità
pubblica, e una nuova tribolazione della vita umana. E non è
scherzo ma verità il dire, che per lui le conoscenze sono sos-
pette e le amicizie pericolose; e che non v'è ora nè luogo dove
qualunque innocente non abbia a temere di essere assaltato, e
sottoposto quivi medesimo, o strascinato altrove, al supplizio
di udire prose senza fine o versi a migliaia, non più sotto scusa
di volersene intendere il suo giudizio, scusa che già lungamente fu costume di assegnare per motivo di tali recitazioni;
ma solo ed espressamente per dar piacere all'autore udendo,
oltre alle lodi necessarie alla fine. In buona coscienza io credo
che in pochissime cose apparisca più, da un lato, la puerilità
della natura umana, ed a quale estremo di cecità, anzi di sto-
lidità, sia condotto l'uomo dall'amor proprio; da altro lato,
quanto innanzi possa l'animo nostro fare illusione a se medesimo; di quello che ciò si dimostri in questo negozio del recitare
gli scritti propri. Perchè, essendo ciascuno consapevole a se
stesso della molestia ineffabile che è a lui sempre l'udire le cose
d'altri; vedendo sbigottire e divenire smorte le persone invitate
ad ascoltare le cose sue, allegare ogni sorte d'impedimenti per
iscusarsi, ed anche fuggire da esso e nascondersi a più potere;
nondimeno con fronte metallica, con perseveranza maravigliosa, come un orso affamato, cerca ed insegue la sua preda
per tutta la città, e sopraggiunta, la tira dove ha destinato. È
durando la recitazione, accorgendosi, prima allo sbadigliare,
poi al distendersi, allo scontorcersi, e a cento altri segni, delle
angosce mortali che prova l'infelice uditore, non per questo si
rimane nè gli dà posa; anzi sempre più fiero e accanito, con-
tinua aringando e gridando per ore, anzi quasi per giorni e per
notti intere, fino a diventarne roco, e finchè, lungo tempo dopo
tramortito l'uditore, non si sente rifinito di forze egli stesso,
benchè non sazio. Nel qual tempo, e nella quale carnificina che
l'uomo fa del suo prossimo, certo è ch'egli prova un piacere

someone who is *not* an author, this practice has become a scourge, a public calamity, one of life's newest hardships. I'm not joking when I say that because of this custom acquaintances have become suspect and friendships dangerous. For no matter where an innocent person goes, or when, he must fear being pounced upon and subjected on the spot (or dragged somewhere else) to the agony of hearing interminable prose or verses by the thousand. No longer under the pretext of soliciting the listener's opinion, which used to be the motive behind such readings, but rather solely and expressly to make the author happy by having someone listen to him, not to speak of the required praises at the end. In all good conscience, I believe there are very few things that reveal the puerility of human nature and the extreme blindness, indeed stupidity, to which self-love leads a man—and which also reveal the illusions we have about ourselves—as does this business of reciting one's own writings. For we are all aware of the unspeakable annoyance we feel when listening to someone else's work. And yet even when an author sees that those he has invited to a reading are terrified, pale with fright, and desperate with excuses, and even when they run and hide from him, still the relentless iron-browed author goes around town seeking and tracking down his prey like a hungry bear. Having caught them, he then leads them to his chosen destination. And during the reading itself, his unhappy audience soon begins to yawn and stretch, twist and turn, giving dozens of signs of their mortal agony—but not for *this* does he stop, nor does he allow any respite. On the contrary, growing still more fierce and relentless, he goes on yelling and haranguing for hours, and for days and nights, until finally he becomes hoarse and has exhausted (long after his stupefied listener) all his energy, though not his enthusiasm. And all during this carnage, he doubtless feels an almost superhuman, paradisiacal pleasure. People do, after all,

quasi sovrumano e di paradiso: poichè veggiamo che le persone lasciano per questo tutti gli altri piaceri, dimenticano il
sonno e il cibo, e spariscono loro dagli occhi la vita e il mondo.
E questo piacere consiste in una ferma credenza che l'uomo ha,
di destare ammirazione e di dar piacere a chi ode: altrimenti il
medesimo gli tornerebbe recitare al deserto, che alle persone.
Ora, come ho detto, quale sia il piacere di chi ode (pensata-
mente dico sempre ode, e non ascolta), lo sa per esperienza
ciascuno, e colui che recita lo vede; e io so ancora, che molti
eleggerebbero, prima che un piacere simile, qualche grave pena corporale. Fino gli scritti più belli e di maggior prezzo, reci-
tandoli il proprio autore, diventano di qualità di uccidere an-
noiando: al qual proposito notava un filologo mio amico, che se
è vero che Ottavia, udendo Virgilio leggere il sesto dell'*Eneide*,
fosse presa da uno svenimento, è credibile che le accadesse ciò,
non tanto per la memoria, come dicono, del figliuolo Marcello,
quanto per la noia del sentir leggere.

Tale è l'uomo. E questo vizio ch'io dico, sì barbaro e sì ridico-
lo, e contrario al senso di creatura razionale, è veramente un
morbo della specie umana: perchè non v'è nazione così gentile,
nè condizione alcuna d'uomini, nè secolo, a cui questa peste
non sia comune. Italiani, Francesi, Inglesi, Tedeschi; uomini
canuti, savissimi nelle altre cose, pieni d'ingegno e di valore;
uomini espertissimi della vita sociale, compitissimi di modi,
amanti di notare le sciocchezze e di motteggiarle; tutti diventano bambini crudeli nelle occasioni di recitare le cose loro. E
come è questo vizio de' tempi nostri, così fu di quelli d'Orazio,
al quale parve già insopportabile; e di quelli di Marziale, che
dimandato da uno perchè non gli leggesse i suoi versi, rispon-
deva: per non udire i tuoi: e così anche fu della migliore età della Grecia, quando, come si racconta, Diogene cinico, trovandosi in compagnia d'altri, tutti moribondi dalla noia, ad una di
tali lezioni, e vedendo nelle mani dell'autore, alla fine del libro,

put aside all other pleasures for the sake of this one; they forget about food and sleep; life and the world vanish from their sight. This pleasure consists in man's firm belief that he is arousing admiration and giving pleasure to whoever hears him. Otherwise he might just as well recite to the desert. Now, as I've said, everyone knows from his own experience—and those who give readings can see for themselves—the "pleasure" felt by the person who hears (I deliberately say "hears" instead of "listens"). And yet I'm sure most would sooner choose some grave corporal punishment before a pleasure such as this. Even when the finest and most esteemed writings are read by their authors, they are liable to kill with boredom. In this regard, a philologist friend of mine has noted that if Octavia really did faint when she heard Vergil read the Sixth Book of *The Aeneid*, it's likely that this was caused no more by the memory of her son Marcellus (as is often claimed) than by the boredom of hearing Vergil read.[8]

Such is man. And the vice I speak of, so uncouth and absurd, so contrary to any creature's rational sense, is truly a widespread disease. For there is no nation so civilized, nor age nor human condition, to which this pestilence is not common. Italians, Frenchmen, Germans, Englishmen, gray-haired men terribly wise in all other matters, men of genius and worth, of impeccable social behavior, of highly refined sensibility who love to observe and scoff at foolishness—*all* become cruel children when reciting their own works. As in our own age, this vice was also present in the days of Horace, to whom even then it seemed insufferable.[9] And in the days of Martial who, when asked by someone why he would not read his verses, replied: "So that I won't have to hear yours!"[10] And even in Greece's Golden Age, as the story goes, the cynic Diogenes once was among a group of people all dying of boredom during such a reading; when Diogenes saw the bright blank paper

comparire il chiaro della carta, disse: fate cuore, amici; veggo terra.

Ma oggi la cosa è venuta a tale, che gli uditori, anche forzati, a fatica possono bastare alle occorrenze degli autori. Onde alcuni miei conoscenti, uomini industriosi, considerato questo punto, e persuasi che il recitare i componimenti propri sia uno de' bisogni della natura umana, hanno pensato di provvedere a questo, e ad un tempo di volgerlo, come si volgono tutti i bisogni pubblici, ad utilità particolare. Al quale effetto in breve apriranno una scuola o accademia ovvero ateneo di ascoltazione; dove, a qualunque ora del giorno e della notte, essi, o persone stipendiate da loro, ascolteranno chi vorrà leggere a prezzi determinati: che saranno per la prosa, la prima ora, uno scudo, la seconda due, la terza quattro, la quarta otto, e così crescendo con progressione aritmetica. Per la poesia il doppio. Per ogni passo letto, volendo tornare a leggerlo, come accade, una lira il verso. Addormentandosi l'ascoltante, sarà rimessa al lettore la terza parte del prezzo debito. Per convulsioni, sincopi, ed altri accidenti leggeri o gravi, che avenissero all'una parte o all'altra nel tempo delle letture, la scuola sarà fornita di essenze e di medicine, che si dispenseranno gratis. Così rendendosi materia di lucro una cosa finora infruttifera, che sono gli orecchi, sarà aperta una nuova strada all'industria, con aumento della ricchezza generale.

XXI

Parlando, non si prova piacere che sia vivo e durevole, se non quanto ci è permesso discorrere di noi medesimi, e delle cose nelle quali siamo occupati, o che ci appartengono in qualche modo. Ogni altro discorso in poca d'ora viene a noia; e questo, ch'è piacevole a noi, è tedio mortale a chi l'ascolta. Non

at the end of the book in the reader's hands, he said: "Take heart, my friends! Land in sight!" [11]

But today the problem has reached such proportions that listeners, even when forced, just barely satisfy the needs of authors. Wherefore some acquaintances of mine, industrious men mindful of this problem and convinced that reading one's own work is a necessity of human nature, have thought to meet this need and at the same time turn it, as all public needs are turned, to personal advantage. In short, they are going to open a school or academy—a kind of athenaeum of auditing—where at any hour of the day or night they or persons employed by them will listen to anyone who wants to read, at predetermined prices. For prose it will be one scudo for the first hour, two for the second, four for the third, eight for the fourth, and so on according to mathematical progression. For poetry, twice the price. For re-reading a passage already covered (which sometimes happens) one lira per line. If the listener falls asleep, one third the due fee shall be remitted to the reader. For convulsions, fainting spells, and other accidents slight and serious that might occur during the course of the reading, the school will be supplied with ointments and medicines to be dispensed free of charge. By thus capitalizing on materials that till now have never shown a profit, namely the human ears, a new path in industry will be opened, increasing the general wealth.

XXI

Talking gives us no vital lasting pleasure except to the extent that we are allowed to talk about ourselves and things we are involved in or which pertain to us in some way. Any other subject becomes boring in less than an hour's time. And although *we* may enjoy talking about ourselves, it is fatally tedious to the

si acquista titolo di amabile, se non a prezzo di patimenti: perchè amabile, conversando, non è se non quegli che gratifica all'amor proprio degli altri, e che, in primo luogo, ascolta assai e tace assai, cosa per lo più noiosissima; poi lascia che gli altri parlino di se e delle cose proprie quanto hanno voglia; anzi li mette in ragionamenti di questa sorte, e parla egli stesso di cose tali; finchè si trovano, al partirsi, quelli contentissimi di se, ed egli annoiatissimo di loro. Perchè, in somma, se la miglior compagnia è quella dalla quale noi partiamo più soddisfatti di noi medesimi, segue ch'ella è appresso a poco quella che noi lasciamo più annoiata. La conchiusione è, che nella conversazione, e in qualunque colloquio dove il fine non sia che intertenersi parlando, quasi inevitabilmente il piacere degli uni è noia degli altri, nè si può sperare se non che annoiarsi o rincrescere, ed è gran fortuna partecipare di questo e di quello ugualmente.

XXII

Assai difficile mi pare a decidere se sia o più contrario ai primi principii della costumatezza il parlare di se lungamente e per abito, o più raro un uomo esente da questo vizio.

XXIII

Quello che si dice comunemente, che la vita è una rappresentazione scenica, si verifica soprattutto in questo, che il mondo parla costantissimamente in una maniera, ed opera costantissimamente in un'altra. Della quale commedia oggi essendo tutti recitanti, perchè tutti parlano a un modo, e nessuno quasi spettatore, perchè il vano linguaggio del mondo non inganna che i fanciulli e gli stolti, segue che tale rappresentazione è di-

person listening. One becomes "likable" only at the cost of much suffering, for a likable person is one whose conversation gratifies the self-esteem of others, one who first of all *listens* a lot and is quiet most of the time—which is incredibly boring. He lets others talk about themselves and their personal affairs as much as they like. Indeed he draws them into discussions of this kind and talks about whatever interests others, so that when they finally leave they feel totally satisfied with themselves and he feels totally bored with them. For if the best kind of company is really the kind we leave feeling most satisfied with ourselves, it follows that this is more or less the kind of company that's most bored when we leave. The result is that in conversation and discussions of any sort, where the only purpose is to pass the time talking, almost inevitably one man's pleasure is another man's boredom. Nor can one hope to be anything other than boring or bored, and it's a great stroke of luck to get equal doses of both.

XXII

I find it awfully difficult to determine if the habit of talking about oneself at length runs contrary to the basic rules of propriety, or if instead the man exempt from this vice is rare.

XXIII

The commonplace expression that life is nothing but a play is verified above all in this: the world speaks absolutely consistently in one way and acts absolutely consistently in another. Everyone today is an actor in this drama. And since everyone recites the same part while precious few play the role of spectator, and since the vain language of the world deceives only children and dolts, this drama has consequently become an

venuta cosa compiutamente inetta, noia e fatica senza causa.
Però sarebbe impresa degna del nostro secolo quella di rendere
la vita finalmente un'azione non simulata ma vera, e di concili-
are per la prima volta al mondo la famosa discordia tra i detti e i
fatti. La quale, essendo i fatti, per esperienza oramai bastante,
conosciuti immutabili, e non convenendo che gli uomini si af-
fatichino più in cerca dell'impossibile, resterebbe che fosse ac-
cordata con quel mezzo che è, ad un tempo, unico e facilissi-
mo, benchè fino a oggi intentato: e questo è, mutare i detti, e
chiamare una volta le cose coi loro nomi.

XXIV

O io m'inganno, o rara è nel nostro secolo quella persona
lodata generalmente, le cui lodi non sieno cominciate dalla sua
propria bocca. Tanto è l'egoismo, e tanta l'invidia e l'odio che
gli uomini portano gli uni agli altri, che volendo acquistar
nome, non basta far cose lodevoli, ma bisogna lodarle, o trovare, che torna lo stesso, alcuno che in tua vece le predichi e le
magnifichi di continuo, intonandole con gran voce negli orecchi del pubblico, per costringere le persone sì mediante l'esempio, e sì coll'ardire e colla perseveranza, a ripetere parte di
quelle lodi. Spontaneamente non isperare che facciano motto,
per grandezza di valore che tu dimostri, per bellezza d'opere
che tu facci. Mirano e tacciono eternamente; e, potendo, im-
pediscono che altri non vegga. Chi vuole innalzarsi, quantunque per virtù vera, dia bando alla modestia. Ancora in questa
parte il mondo è simile alle donne: con verecondia e con riser-
bo da lui non si ottiene nulla.

utterly insipid, boring, and senseless toil. Therefore, an under-
taking worthy of our age would be to make life finally an *action*, real rather than simulated, and to resolve for the first time
in history the notorious discrepancy between words and
deeds. Since experience has sufficiently shown that deeds are
irreversible, and since it's impractical for men to keep exhaust-
ing themselves in search of the impossible, this discrepancy
might be resolved by a method at once unique and extremely
simple, though until today untested—that is, by changing our
speech habits and for once calling things by their real names.

XXIV

I may be wrong, but it seems rare in our age to find a widely
praised person whose own mouth is not the source of that
praise. Man's egoism is so great, and the envy and hatred men
feel against one another so intense, that for a man to make a
name for himself it isn't enough simply to *do* laudable things—
he must praise them as well. Or else you must find someone to
do it for you (which amounts to the same thing), someone who
will continually declaim and extol your works. By pouring
boisterous praises into the public ear, he forces people by his
example and through his passion and perseverance to reiterate
some of this praise. Don't expect the public to stir themselves
of their own accord out of regard for your personal excellence,
or because the things you make are beautiful. They will look
on and remain eternally silent; and when they can, they will
prevent others from seeing it. A man who wishes to elevate
himself has to forego modesty, even if he is inspired by real virtue. In this respect, too, the world is like a woman: modesty
and discretion win a man nothing.

XXV

Nessuno è sì compiutamente disingannato del mondo, nè lo conosce sì addentro, nè tanto l'ha in ira, che guardato un tratto da esso con benignità, non se gli senta in parte riconciliato; come nessuno è conosciuto da noi sì malvagio, che salutandoci cortesemente, non ci apparisca meno malvagio che innanzi. Le quali osservazioni vagliono a dimostrare la debolezza dell'uomo, non a giustificare nè i malvagi nè il mondo.

XXVI

L'inesperto della vita, e spesso anche l'esperto, in sui primi momenti che si conosce colto da qualche infortunio, massime dove egli non abbia colpa, se pure gli corrono all'animo gli amici e i familiari, o in generale gli uomini, non aspetta da loro altro che commiserazione e conforto, e, per tacere qui d'aiuto, che gli abbiano o più amore o più riguardo che innanzi; nè cosa alcuna è sì lungi dal cadergli in pensiero, come vedersi, a causa della sventura occorsagli, quasi degradato nella società, diventato agli occhi del mondo quasi reo di qualche misfatto, venuto in disgrazia degli amici, gli amici e i conoscenti da tutti i lati in fuga, e di lontano rallegrarsi della cosa, e porre lui in derisione. Similmente, accadendogli qualche prosperità, uno de' primi pensieri che gli nascono, è di avere a dividere la sua gioia cogli amici, e che forse di maggior contento riesca la cosa a loro che a lui; nè gli sa venire in capo che debbano, all'annunzio del suo caso prospero, i volti de' suoi cari distorcersi ed oscurarsi, e alcuno sbigottire; molti sforzarsi in principio di non credere, poi di rappiccinire nell'estimazione sua, e nella loro propria e degli altri, il suo nuovo bene; in certi, a causa di questo, intepidirsi l'amicizia, in altri mutarsi in odio; finalmente non pochi mettere ogni loro potere ed opera per ispogliarlo di esso bene. Così

XXV

It makes no difference how disenchanted a man is with the world, or how deeply he knows it, or how much it enrages him, for if the world suddenly smiles on him, he feels himself partially reconciled with it. Likewise, no matter how wicked we consider someone to be, if he greets us in a friendly way he is bound to seem less wicked than before. Such observations help demonstrate man's weakness; they don't justify his world or his wickedness.

XXVI

Say that a worldly wise man, or even one who is not, finds himself suddenly trapped by some misfortune. Even if his friends and acquaintances, or people in general, take pity on him, he at first expects from them really nothing more than solace or commiseration, especially when he's not at fault for his misfortune. And, assistance apart, he expects them either to feel more love or show more consideration for him than before. Nothing is farther from his thoughts than seeing himself degraded in society because of his misfortune, so he is surprised when the world looks upon him almost as a criminal. He is disgraced among his friends; both friends and acquaintances desert and ridicule him, laughing from afar at his misfortune. On the other hand, when he has a stroke of good fortune, one of his first thoughts is to share his happiness with his friends, thinking they might enjoy the good news even more than he. Consequently, he feels at a total loss when he sees what follows the announcement of his good fortune. Those dear to him inevitably begin to brood and smirk, some genuinely appalled; at first many try hard to discount his new-found prosperity, then seek to minimize its importance not just in his own eyes but also to themselves and others. Such good

è l'immaginazione dell'uomo ne' suoi concetti, e la ragione stessa, naturalmente lontana e aborrente dalla realtà della vita.

XXVII

Nessun maggior segno d'essere poco filosofo e poco savio, che volere savia e filosofica tutta la vita.

XXVIII

Il genere umano e, dal solo individuo in fuori, qualunque minima porzione di esso, si divide in due parti: gli uni usano prepotenza, e gli altri la soffrono. Nè legge nè forza alcuna, nè progresso di filosofia nè di civiltà potendo impedire che uomo nato o da nascere non sia o degli uni o degli altri, resta che chi può eleggere, elegga. Vero è che non tutti possono, nè sempre.

XXIX

Nessuna professione è sì sterile come quella delle lettere. Pure tanto è al mondo il valore dell'impostura, che con l'aiuto di essa anche le lettere diventano fruttifere. L'impostura è anima, per dir così, della vita sociale, ed arte senza cui veramente nessun'arte e nessuna facoltà, considerandola in quanto agli effetti suoi negli animi umani, è perfetta. Sempre che tu esaminerai la fortuna di due persone che sieno l'una di valor vero in qualunque cosa, l'altra di valor falso, tu troverai che questa è più fortunata di quella; anzi il più delle volte questa fortunata, e quella senza fortuna. L'impostura vale e fa effetto anche senza il vero; ma il vero senza lei non può nulla. Nè ciò nasce,

fortune sometimes dampens friendship, sometimes turns friendship to hatred. Eventually, more than a few will make every effort to strip him of his prosperity. So much for man's imagination and for human reason—both naturally alien to, and repulsed by, life's realities.

XXVII

There's no greater sign of being a poor philosopher and wise man than wanting all of life to be wise and philosophical.

XXVIII

The human race, from the individual on up, and even in its smallest units, is split into two camps: the bullies and the bullied. Neither law nor force of any kind, nor advancements in civilization and philosophy, can prevent men now or in the future from belonging to one of these two camps. So, he who can choose, must choose. Although not everyone is able, nor is the choice always available.

XXIX

No profession is so sterile as that of letters. But the world puts such a high value on deceit that with its help even letters becomes fruitful. Fraudulence is as it were the soul of social life. Given its effects on the human mind, no art or human faculty is really perfect without it. If you were to study the histories of two people—the one honest in all things, the other deceitful—you would always find the latter more fortunate than the former. The honest man is in fact almost entirely barren of good fortune. Artifice lacking truth is valuable and effective, but truth lacking artifice is impotent. I don't think this is due to

credo io, da mala inclinazione della nostra specie, ma perchè essendo il vero sempre troppo povero e difettivo, è necessaria all'uomo in ciascuna cosa, per dilettarlo o per muoverlo, parte d'illusione e di prestigio, e promettere assai più e meglio che non si può dare. La natura medesima è impostora verso l'uomo, nè gli rende la vita amabile o sopportabile, se non per mezzo principalmente d'immaginazione e d'inganno.

XXX

Come suole il genere umano, biasimando le cose presenti, lodare le passate, così la più parte de' viaggiatori, mentre viaggiano, sono amanti del loro soggiorno nativo, e lo preferiscono con una specie d'ira a quelli dove si trovano. Tornati al luogo nativo, colla stessa ira lo pospongono a tutti gli altri luoghi dove sono stati.

XXXI

In ogni paese i vizi e i mali universali degli uomini e della società umana, sono notati come particolari del luogo. Io non sono mai stato in parte dov'io non abbia udito: qui le donne sono vane e incostanti, leggono poco, e sono male istruite; qui il pubblico è curioso de' fatti altrui, ciarliero molto e maldicente; qui i danari, il favore e la viltà possono tutti; qui regna l'invidia, e le amicizie sono poco sincere; e così discorrendo; come se altrove le cose procedessero in altro modo. Gli uomini sono miseri per necessità, e risoluti di credersi miseri per accidente.

XXXII

Venendo innanzi nella cognizione pratica della vita, l'uomo rimette ogni giorno di quella severità per la quale i giovani,

the wicked inclinations of our species, but rather because in everything he does man needs some illusion and glamour, since truth is always too flawed and impoverished. Illusion pleases and inspires him. He lives for the promise of something more, and better, than what the world can actually give. Even Nature is deceitful toward man: it makes life congenial and tolerable only through imagination and artifice.

XXX

As mankind usually praises the things of the past while disparaging those of the present, so most travelers love their native land while traveling, preferring it with a kind of vengeance over the places they visit. Then once they return to their native place, with the same vengeance they judge it inferior to all the other places they have seen.

XXXI

Each country thinks that the universal vices and evils of men and society are peculiar to itself. I hear the same complaints wherever I go: the women here are vain and fickle, they read little and are poorly educated; the people here are gossipy and backbiting, always nosing into other people's business; here money, favors, and cowardice are what count; here envy reigns and friendships are hardly sincere, and so forth. As if things were any different elsewhere. Men are miserable by necessity, yet determined to think themselves miserable by accident.

XXXII

As a man learns more about the practicalities of life, he begins to surrender each day some of the severity that young

sempre cercando perfezione, e aspettando trovarne, e misu-
rando tutte le cose a quell'idea della medesima che hanno
nell'animo, sono sì difficili a perdonare i difetti, ed a concedere
stima alle virtù scarse e manchevoli, ed ai pregi di poco momento, che occorrono loro negli uomini. Poi, vedendo come
tutto è imperfetto, e persuadendosi che non v'è meglio al mondo di quel poco buono che essi disprezzano, e che quasi nessuna cosa o persona è stimabile veramente, a poco a poco, can-
giata misura, e ragguagliando ciò che viene loro avanti, non
più al perfetto, ma al vero, si assuefanno a perdonare liberal-
mente, e a fare stima di ogni virtù mediocre, di ogni ombra di
valore, di ogni piccola facoltà che trovano; tanto che finalmente
paiono loro lodevoli molte cose e molte persone che da prima
sarebbero parute loro appena sopportabili. La cosa va tant'oltre, che, dove a principio non avevano quasi attitudine a sentire stima, in progresso di tempo diventano quasi inabili a disprezzare; maggiormente quanto sono più ricchi d'intelligenza.
Perchè in vero l'essere molto disprezzante ed incontentabile
passata la prima giovinezza, non è buon segno: e questi tali
debbono, o per poco intelletto, o certo per poca esperienza,
non aver conosciuto il mondo; ovvero essere di quegli sciocchi
che disprezzano altrui per grande stima che hanno di se medesimi. In fine apparisce poco probabile, ma è vero, nè viene a
significare altro che l'estrema bassezza delle cose umane il dire,
che l'uso del mondo insegna più a pregiare che a dispregiare.

XXXIII

Gl'ingannatori mediocri, e generalmente le donne, credono
sempre che le loro frodi abbiano avuto effetto, e che le persone
vi sieno restate colte: ma i più astuti dubitano, conoscendo
meglio da un lato le difficoltà dell'arte, dall'altro la potenza,
e come quel medesimo che vogliono essi, cioè ingannare, sia

men often show. The young always seek perfection, which they always expect to find, and they measure all things against their own *idea* of perfection; therefore at first they are most reluctant to excuse human shortcomings and to respect those few imperfect virtues and unexceptional merits they find among men. Later, however, when they see how imperfect everything is, they begin to realize that the little bit of goodness they scorn is really the best the world has to offer, and that hardly anyone or anything is truly praiseworthy. As their standards change, they become less concerned with perfectability and more concerned with plain truth. They learn to forgive, they learn to respect *ordinary* virtues, mere shadows of value, even the slightest trace of substance. So that many of the things and people they would hardly have tolerated before, in the end seem praiseworthy. So much so that, whereas at first they were almost incapable of feeling respect, with the passing of time they become almost incapable of feeling contempt, especially if they are more intelligent than others. For it is a bad sign for a man to remain scornful and scrupulous beyond his early youth. Those who do lack either the intelligence or experience necessary for knowing the world; or else they are the kinds of fools who scorn others out of excessive self-esteem. Unlikely as it seems, it is true that, as the saying goes, experience teaches us to praise rather than to disparage, which is nothing more than an expression of the extremely low state of human affairs.

XXXIII

Second-rate swindlers, and women in general, always think that their tricks have worked and that they have trapped their victims; but the really smart ones distrust this. For not only are they more aware of the difficulties and the power of their art, but they also realize that their objective, namely to deceive, is

voluto da ognuno; le quali due cause ultime fanno che spesso
l'ingannatore riesce ingannato. Oltre che questi tali non isti-
mano gli altri così poco intendenti, come suole immaginarli chi
intende poco.

XXXIV

I giovani assai comunemente credono rendersi amabili, fin-
gendosi malinconici. E forse, quando è finta, la malinconia per
breve spazio può piacere, massime alle donne. Ma vera, è fug-
gita da tutto il genere umano; e al lungo andare non piace e
non è fortunata nel commercio degli uomini se non l'allegria:
perchè finalmente, contro a quello che si pensano i giovani, il
mondo, e non ha il torto, ama non di piangere, ma di ridere.

XXXV

In alcuni luoghi tra civili e barbari, come è, per esempio,
Napoli, è osservabile più che altrove una cosa che in qualche
modo si verifica in tutti i luoghi: cioè che l'uomo riputato senza
danari, non è stimato appena uomo; creduto denaroso, è sempre in pericolo della vita. Dalla qual cosa nasce, che in sì fatti
luoghi è necessario, come vi si pratica generalmente, pigliare
per partito di rendere lo stato proprio in materia di danari un
mistero; acciocchè il pubblico non sappia se ti dee disprezzare
o ammazzare; onde tu non sii se non quello che sono gli uomini ordinariamente, mezzo disprezzato e mezzo stimato, e
quando voluto nuocere e quando lasciato stare.

XXXVI

Molti vogliono e condursi teco vilmente, e che tu ad un
tempo, sotto pena del loro odio, da un lato sii tanto accorto,

everyone's objective—thus the deceiver himself is often de- ceived. Moreover, smart tricksters never assume others to be as dumb as dumb tricksters imagine them to be.

XXXIV

Young men quite commonly think they make themselves more likable by acting melancholy. And in fact it is possible for melancholy, when pretended, to give pleasure for a short while, especially to women. But true melancholy is shunned by all mankind. And in the long run only cheerfulness is pleas- ing and profitable in human affairs. For in the end, contrary to what young men think, the world—and it is not wrong—loves laughter more than tears.

XXXV

In places that still lie somewhere between civilization and barbarism—Naples, for example—one more often sees some- thing that can be found everywhere in some form or other. That is, a man known to be penniless is hardly considered a man at all; if thought wealthy, however, his life is constantly in danger. Consequently, you must be sure to keep your financial circumstances a mystery (the standard practice in such places) so that the public won't know whether to scorn you or kill you. In which case you are really no different from what men usu- ally are: half-scorned and half-esteemed, sometimes hurt and sometimes left alone.

XXXVI

Many men, even while treating you badly, hope that under pain of their hatred you will be smart enough not to stand in

che tu non dia impedimento alla loro viltà, dall'altro non li conoschi per vili.

XXXVII

Nessuna qualità umana è più intollerabile nella vita ordinaria, nè in fatti tollerata meno, che l'intolleranza.

XXXVIII

Come l'arte dello schermire è inutile quando combattono insieme due schermitori uguali nella perizia, perchè l'uno non ha più vantaggio dall'altro, che se fossero ambedue imperiti; così spessissime volte accade che gli uomini sono falsi e malvagi gratuitamente, perchè si scontrano in altrettanta malvagità e simulazione, di modo che la cosa ritorna a quel medesimo che se l'una e l'altra parte fosse stata sincera e retta. Non è dubbio che, al far de' conti, la malvagità e la doppiezza non sono utili se non quando o vanno congiunte alla forza, o si abbattono ad una malvagità o astuzia minore, ovvero alla bontà. Il quale ultimo caso è raro; il secondo, in quanto a malvagità, non è comune; perchè gli uomini, la maggior parte, sono malvagi a un modo, poco più o meno. Però non è calcolabile quante volte potrebbero essi, facendo bene gli uni agli altri, ottenere con facilità quel medesimo che ottengono con gran fatica, o anche non ottengono, facendo ovvero sforzandosi di far male.

XXXIX

Baldassar Castiglione nel *Cortegiano* assegna molto convenientemente la cagione perchè sogliano i vecchi lodare il tempo in cui furono giovani, e biasimare il presente. "La causa adunque" dice "di questa falsa opinione nei vecchi, estimo io per me

their way. Yet at the same time they don't want you to think them mean.

XXXVII

No human trait is more intolerable in everyday life, nor in fact less tolerated, than intolerance.

XXXVIII

The art of fencing is a useless exercise when two fencers of equal skill engage each other, since one's advantage over the other is no greater than if they were both unskilled. In the same way, man's lies and wickedness are almost always gratuitous, since they are met by equal measures of duplicity and wickedness, so that things turn out no differently than they would were both parties sincere and honest. Surely in the final reckoning wickedness and duplicity are useful only when joined to force, or when met either by much less wickedness and cunning or by goodness. This last instance is rare. And the case of less wickedness is uncommon, since men—most of them—are wicked more or less to the same degree. Thus it's hard to know how often men might obtain through kindness the very thing they struggle (and sometimes fail) to obtain by acting or trying to act wickedly.

XXXIX

In *The Book of the Courtier*, Balthazar Castiglione very aptly explains why old people usually disparage the present while praising the time when they were young: "Thus in my opinion, the cause of this mistaken notion among old people is that

ch'ella sia perchè gli anni, fuggendo, se ne portan seco molte
comodità, e tra l'altre levano dal sangue gran parte degli spiriti
vitali, onde la complession si muta, e divengon debili gli organi
per i quali l'anima opera le sue virtù. Però dei cuori nostri in
quel tempo, come allo autunno le foglie degli alberi, caggiono i
soavi fiori di contento, e nel luogo dei sereni e chiari pensieri
entra la nubilosa e torbida tristizia, di mille calamità compa-
gnata: di modo che non solamente il corpo, ma l'animo ancora è
infermo, nè dei passati piaceri riserva altro che una tenace memoria, e la immagine di quel caro tempo della tenera età, nella
quale quando ci ritroviamo, ci pare che sempre il cielo e la terra
ed ogni cosa faccia festa e rida intorno agli occhi nostri, e nel
pensiero, come in un delizioso e vago giardino, fiorisca la dolce
primavera d'allegrezza. Onde forse saria utile, quando già
nella fredda stagione comincia il sole della nostra vita, spo-
gliandoci di quei piaceri, andarsene verso l'occaso, perdere insieme con essi ancor la loro memoria, e trovar, come disse Te-
mistocle, un'arte che a scordar insegnasse; perchè tanto sono
fallaci i sensi del corpo nostro, che spesso ingannano ancora il
giudicio della mente. Però parmi che i vecchi siano alla con-
dizion di quelli che partendosi dal porto tengon gli occhi in
terra, e par loro che la nave stia ferma e la riva si parta; e pur è
il contrario, che il porto, e medesimamente il tempo e i piaceri,
restano nel suo stato, e noi con la nave della mortalità fuggendo, n'andiamo l'un dopo l'altro per quel procelloso mare
che ogni cosa assorbe e divora; nè mai più ripiglar terra ci è
concesso, anzi, sempre da contrari venti combattuti, al fine in
qualche scoglio la nave rompemo. Per esser adunque l'animo
senile subietto disproporzionato a molti piaceri, gustar non gli
può; e come ai febbricitanti, quando dai vapori corrotti hanno il
palato guasto, paiono tutti i vini amarissimi, benchè preziosi e
delicati siano, così ai vecchi per la loro indisposizione, alla qual
però non manca il desiderio, paion i piaceri insipidi e freddi e

the fleeting years steal from them most human comforts; they leaven the blood of most of its vital spirits, whereby the constitution is altered and the organs by which the soul exercises its powers grow weak. Hence in our old age the gentle flowers of happiness fall from our hearts as leaves from trees in autumn; and in the place of serene and lucid thoughts there comes but gloomy and cloudy sadness, attended by a thousand ills. So it is that not only the body, but also the mind, grows ever more infirm. Of past pleasures we retain only a lingering memory and the image of that fond time of tender youth in which, even as we look back upon that place once again, heaven and earth and all its creatures seem to be endlessly celebrating, and the sweet springtime of happiness seems to bloom in our thoughts as in a lush and delicate garden. So that when the sun of life enters its wintry season and with its westward descent deprives us of such pleasures, it may perhaps be useful to lose our remembrance of them as well and discover—as Themistocles said—an art that would teach us to forget. For our body's senses are so misleading that they are often wont to beguile the mind's judgment as well. Thus it seems to me that the plight of the aged is similar to that of those who, when departing from the harbor, fix their gaze upon the shore and think that their ship does not move, but that it is the shore that is departing. And yet quite the contrary is true: the harbor, and likewise time and its pleasures, remain fixed while we, one after another, flee on the ship of our mortality, voyaging across that stormy sea that devours and consumes all things. Nor shall we ever be allowed to touch land again; rather, our ship, beaten about by opposing winds, shall in the end scuttle us upon some reef. Since a senile and weathered spirit is unsuited or unfit for most pleasures, it obviously cannot enjoy them. And just as to victims of fever whose palates are spoiled by corrupt vapors all wines, however delicate and precious they may be, seem terribly bitter, so to old people, indisposed as they are,

molto differenti da quelli che già provati aver si ricordano,
benchè i piaceri in se siano i medesimi. Però, sentendosene
privi, si dolgono, e biasimano il tempo presente come malo;
non discernendo che quella mutazione da se e non dal tempo
procede. E, per contrario, recandosi a memoria i passati piaceri, si arrecano ancor il tempo nel quale avuti gli hanno; e però
lo laudano come buono; perchè pare che seco porti un odore di
quello che in esso sentiano quando era presente. Perchè in
effetto gli animi nostri hanno in odio tutte le cose che state
sono compagne de' nostri dispiaceri, ed amano quelle che state
sono compagne dei piaceri".

Così il Castiglione, esponendo con parole non meno belle
che ridondanti, come sogliono i prosatori italiani, un pensiero
verissimo. A confermazione del quale si può considerare che i
vecchi pospongono il presente al passato, non solo nelle cose
che dipendono dall'uomo, ma ancora in quelle che non dipendono, accusandole similmente di essere peggiorate, non tanto,
com'è il vero, in essi e verso di essi, ma generalmente e in se
medesime. Io credo che ognuno si ricordi avere udito da' suoi
vecchi più volte, come mi ricordo io da' miei, che le annate
sono divenute più fredde che non erano, e gl'inverni più lunghi; e che, al tempo loro, già verso il dì di pasqua si solevano
lasciare i panni dell'inverno, e pigliare quelli della state; la qual
mutazione oggi, secondo essi, appena nel mese di maggio, e
talvolta di giugno, si può patire. E non ha molti anni, che fu
cercata seriamente da alcuni fisici la causa di tale supposto
raffreddamento delle stagioni, ed allegato da chi il diboscamen-
mento delle montagne, e da chi non so che altre cose, per ispie-
gare un fatto che non ha luogo: poichè anzi al contrario è cosa,
a cagione d'esempio, notata da qualcuno per diversi passi d'autori antichi, che l'Italia ai tempi romani dovette essere più
fredda che non è ora. Cosa credibilissima anche perchè da altra

pleasures seem cold and insipid, though the desire for pleasure still exists. And although the pleasures themselves remain the same, they yet seem quite different from those that
old people remember having once enjoyed. Feeling thus deprived of such pleasures, they sink into regret and denounce
the present as evil, since they are unable to perceive that the
change lies within themselves, not in time. Instead, they call to
mind the delights of the past and the times when such pleasures were to be had; and they therefore praise the past as
good since it seems to convey a fragrance of the delight they
once felt when it was present. Since, after all, our souls feel
hatred for all things that have companioned our sorrows, and
love for the companion of our delights." [12]

Castiglione's point, expressed in language as beautiful as it is
redundant (a habit among Italian prose writers) is irrefutable.
We can further confirm it by considering how old people prefer
the past to the present in every way, even in things that are not
directly related to them. They insist not only that their own
condition has worsened, which is true enough, but that *things
in general* have deteriorated. I think all of us, myself included,
can recall hearing our elders say that the years are colder than
they used to be and that the winters last longer. That in *their*
day, by Easter Sunday they could put away their winter clothing and begin wearing summer things. Today, according to
them, you have to wait until May, sometimes June, before
changing to summer dress. And it wasn't too long ago that certain physicists were seriously investigating the cause of this
supposed cooling of the seasons; some blamed the deforesta-
tion of the mountains, others offered one reason or another to
explain a phenomenon that is not in fact taking place. Quite
the opposite is happening. Various passages in the ancient authors give us reason to believe that in Roman times Italy must

parte è manifesto per isperienza, e per ragioni naturali, che la
civiltà degli uomini venendo innanzi, rende l'aria, ne' paesi
abitati da essi, di giorno in giorno più mite: il quale effetto è
stato ed è palese singolarmente in America, dove, per così dire,
a memoria nostra, una civiltà matura è succeduta parte a uno
stato barbaro, e parte a mera solitudine. Ma i vecchi, riuscendo
il freddo all'età loro assai più molesto che in gioventù, credono
avvenuto alle cose il cangiamento che provano nello stato proprio, ed immaginano che il calore che va scemando in loro,
scemi nell'aria o nella terra. La quale immaginazione è così fon-
data, che quel medesimo appunto che affermano i nostri vecchi
a noi, affermavano i vecchi, per non dir più, già un secolo e
mezzo addietro, ai contemporanei del Magalotti, il quale nelle
Lettere familiari scriveva: "egli è pur certo che l'ordine antico
delle stagioni par che vada pervertendosi. Qui in Italia è voce e
querela comune, che i mezzi tempi non vi son più; e in questo
smarrimento di confini, non vi è dubbio che il freddo acquista
terreno. Io ho udito dire a mio padre, che in sua gioventù, a
Roma, la mattina di pasqua di resurrezione, ognuno si rivesti-
va da state. Adesso chi non ha bisogno d'impegnar la camici-
uola, vi so dire che si guarda molto bene di non alleggerirsi della minima cosa di quelle ch'ei portava nel cuor dell'inverno".

Questo scriveva il Magalotti in data del 1683. L'Italia sarebbe
più fredda oramai che la Groenlandia, se da quell'anno a questo, fosse venuta continuamente raffreddandosi a quella proporzione che si raccontava allora. È quasi soverchio l'aggiun-
gere che il raffreddamento continuo che si dice aver luogo per
cagioni intrinseche nella massa terrestre, non ha interesse alcuno col presente proposito, essendo cosa, per la sua lentezza,
non sensibile in decine di secoli, non che in pochi anni.

have been colder than it is now, which is entirely credible, especially since experience and natural causes both show that the progress of civilization in certain places actually renders the climate progressively milder. This effect is still most obvious in America where, in our own memory, a mature civilization has followed upon what was once partly a barbarous state and partly a mere wasteland. But because the cold is so much more annoying in old age than in youth, our elders think that the change they feel inside themselves has also affected everything else, and they imagine that the heat diminishing in their bodies is likewise diminishing in the air or inside the earth. This fancy is so deeply rooted that at least a century and a half ago, in Magalotti's time, old people were expressing the same idea we hear today. In his *Lettere Familiari*, Magalotti wrote: "It is indeed certain that the ancient order of the seasons is in the process of reversing itself. Here in Italy the general hail and cry is that moderate temperatures no longer obtain, and that in the confounding of all normal measures there can be no doubt that the cold is winning. I have heard it said to my father that during his youth, in Rome, on Easter morning everyone dressed in summer clothing. Today anyone who can avoid pawning his underwaist had better not do away with even the least of those things he used to wear in the dead of winter." [13]

Magalotti wrote this in 1693. If the cooling process had continued at the same rate remarked upon back then, Italy by now would be colder than Greenland. It's almost superfluous to add that the steady cooling, which is said to be taking place as a result of certain causes inherent to terrestrial mass, has no bearing whatsoever on the present topic. For this is something that happens so slowly that it passes unfelt over the course of centuries, let alone over a few years.

XL

Cosa odiosissima è il parlar molto di se. Ma i giovani, quanto
sono più di natura viva, e di spirito superiore alla mediocrità,
meno sanno guardarsi da questo vizio: e parlano delle cose
proprie con un candore estremo, credendo per certissimo che
chi ode, le curi poco meno che le curano essi. E così facendo,
sono perdonati; non tanto a contemplazione dell'inesperienza,
ma perchè è manifesto il bisogno che hanno d'aiuto, di consiglio e di qualche sfogo di parole alle passioni onde è tem-
pestosa la loro età. Ed anco pare riconosciuto generalmente che
ai giovani si appartenga una specie di diritto di volere il mondo
occupato nei pensieri loro.

XLI

Rade volte è ragione che l'uomo si tenga offeso di cose dette
di lui fuori della sua presenza, o con intenzione che non doves-
sero venirgli alle orecchie: perchè se vorrà ricordarsi, ed esami-
nare diligentemente l'usanza propria, egli non ha così caro
amico, e non ha personaggio alcuno in tanta venerazione, al
quale non fosse per fare gravissimo dispiacere d'intendere
molte parole e molti discorsi che fuggono a lui di bocca intorno
ad esso amico o ad esso personaggio assente. Da un lato l'amor
proprio è così a dismisura tenero, e così cavilloso, che quasi è
impossibile che una parola detta di noi fuori della presenza
nostra, se ci è recata fedelmente, non ci paia indegna o poco
degna di noi, e non ci punga; dall'altro è indicibile quanto la
nostra usanza sia contraria al precetto del non fare agli altri
quello che non vogliamo fatto a noi, e quanta libertà di parlare
in proposito d'altri sia giudicata innocente.

XL

It is absolutely hateful to talk too much about oneself. But with young men, the more vital they are and the more their spirit transcends the ordinary, the less they know how to avoid this vice. They speak with extreme candor, certain that the person listening will share their intense concern for what they say. We can forgive them for acting this way, not so much in light of their inexperience, but because of their obvious need for help and advice, and for some verbal outlet for the stormy passions of their age. And it also seems generally acknowledged that the young possess a kind of right to ask that the world pay attention to what they are thinking.

XLI

It is seldom right for a man to take offense at things said either in his absence or with the intention that they never reach his ears. For if a man stops to examine his own conduct, he will find that he has no friend so dear, and holds no personage in such high regard, that he has not often been on the verge of seriously offending one or the other by letting certain words and remarks slip from his mouth. On the one hand, self-love is so extremely fragile and captious that anything said of us in our absence, if faithfully reported, is bound to seem undeserved or inappropriate, so that it's sure to sting us. On the other hand, it's unspeakable how much our own conduct runs contrary to the rule of doing unto others as we would have others do unto us, and how innocently we regard our freedom to talk about other people.

XLII

Nuovo sentimento è quello che prova l'uomo di età di poco più di venticinque anni, quando, come a un tratto, si conosce tenuto da molti de' suoi compagni più provetto di loro, e, considerando, si avvede che v'è in fatti al mondo una quantità di persone giovani più di lui, avvezzo a stimarsi collocato, senza contesa alcuna, come nel supremo grado della giovinezza, e se anche si reputava inferiore agli altri in ogni altra cosa, credersi non superato nella gioventù da nessuno; perchè i più giovani di lui, ancora poco più che fanciulli, e rade volte suoi compagni, non erano parte, per dir così, del mondo. Allora incomincia egli a sentire come il pregio della giovinezza, stimato da lui quasi proprio della sua natura e della sua essenza, tanto che appena gli sarebbe stato possibile d'immaginare se stesso diviso da quello, non è dato se non a tempo; e diventa sollecito di così fatto pregio, sì quanto alla cosa in se, e sì quanto all'opinione altrui. Certamente di nessuno che abbia passata l'età di venticinque anni, subito dopo la quale incomincia il fiore della gioventù a perdere, si può dire con verità, se non fosse di qualche stupido, ch'egli non abbia esperienza di sventure; perchè se anco la sorte fosse stata prospera ad alcuno in ogni cosa, pure questi, passato il detto tempo, sarebbe conscio a se stesso di una sventura grave ed amara fra tutte l'altre, e forse più grave ed amara a chi sia dalle altre parti meno sventurato; cioè della decadenza o della fine della cara sua gioventù.

XLIII

Uomini insigni per probità sono al mondo quelli dai quali, avendo familiarità con loro, tu puoi, senza sperare servigio alcuno, non temere alcun disservigio.

XLII

It's a queer feeling for a man in his mid-twenties to find out, rather unexpectedly, that many of his companions think of him as an older man. Considering this, he begins to realize that there are after all a good number of people in the world younger than he, though he prefers to think himself at the very peak of his youth. Even if he considers himself inferior to others in everything else, he still cannot believe that anyone is more *youthful*; for those younger than he, who are still practically children and seldom his companions, are not as it were part of his world. He then begins to feel that the *honor* of youth—his youth being so intimately tied to his own nature, to his very essence, that he cannot possibly imagine himself divorced from it—is an honor given only once. And he becomes as solicitous of this honor as of youth itself and of other people's opinions. Since the flower of youth begins to wilt as soon as a man passes twenty-five, no one (certain idiots excepted) can truthfully say that such a man has never experienced misfortune. Because even if fate has been kind to him in every other way, even he, once past this age, will become personally aware of one grave and bitter misfortune among all the others. A misfortune perhaps all the more serious and bitter for someone who is lucky in every other respect—I mean the decline and demise of his beloved youth.

XLIII

Men whom the world recognizes for their moral integrity are those from whom you need fear no disservice once you get to know them, even while you expect no favors from them.

XLIV

Se tu interroghi le persone sottoposte ad un magistrato, o a un qualsivoglia ministro del governo, circa le qualità e i portamenti di quello, massime nell'ufficio; anche concordando le risposte nei fatti, tu ritroverai gran dissensione nell'interpretarli; e quando pure le interpretazioni fossero conformi, infinitamente discordi saranno i giudizi, biasimando gli uni quelle cose che gli altri esalteranno. Solo circa l'astenersi o no dalla roba d'altri e del pubblico, non troverai due persone che, accordandosi nel fatto, discordino o nell'interpretarlo o nel farne giudizio, e che ad una voce, semplicemente, non lodino il magistrato dell'astinenza, o per la qualità contraria, non lo condannino. E pare che in somma il buono e il cattivo magistrato non si conosca nè si misuri da altro che dall'articolo dei danari; anzi magistrato buono vaglia lo stesso che astinente, cattivo lo stesso che cupido. E che l'ufficiale pubblico possa disporre a suo modo della vita, dell'onestà e d'ogni altra cosa dei cittadini; e di qualunque suo fatto trovare non solo scusa ma lode; purchè non tocchi i danari. Quasi che gli uomini, discordando in tutte l'altre opinioni, non convengano che nella stima della moneta: o quasi che i danari in sostanza sieno l'uomo; e non altro che i danari: cosa che veramente pare per mille indizi che sia tenuta dal genere umano per assioma costante, massime ai tempi nostri. Al qual proposito diceva un filosofo francese del secolo passato: i politici antichi parlavano sempre di costumi e di virtù; i moderni non parlano d'altro che di commercio e di moneta. Ed è gran ragione, soggiunge qualche studente di economia politica, o allievo delle gazzette in filosofia: perchè le virtù e i buoni costumi non possono stare in piedi senza il fondamento dell'industria; la quale provvedendo alle necessità giornaliere, e rendendo agiato e sicuro il vivere a tutti gli ordini di persone, renderà stabili le virtù, e proprie dell'universale.

XLIV

Talk to people who have come before a magistrate or any kind of government official and ask them about his conduct and abilities, especially with regard to his office. Even if their answers are factually consistent, they will interpret the facts in different ways; and even if their interpretations agree, their final judgments will be incredibly inconsistent, some people criticizing what others extol. The only time people all agree on the facts, as well as in their interpretations and final opinions, is when it has to do with a bureaucrat's meddling in someone's financial affairs or in public business. In this instance, each and every one will either praise the bureaucrat's self-control or damn him for lacking it. It seems, in effect, that an official is recognized and judged good or bad only with regard to money: the self-restrained official is a good official, the greedy official a bad one. A public functionary can apparently do as he likes with citizens' lives, their honesty, and everything else; and no matter what he does, the people will not only pardon him, they will praise him, providing their money is not at stake. As if men, holding different opinions on everything else, were united only in their respect for money, as if money and nothing else were what constitutes man's essence. Everything indicates that this is what mankind takes as its working assumption, especially in our own time. In this regard, a French philosopher of the last century said that ancient politicians always talked about custom and virtue, whereas moderns talk only about commerce and money.[14] Certain political economists and readers of philosophy journals support this notion, since, as they say, civilized customs and virtues can be built only on the foundation of industry, and industry stabilizes virtue on a universal scale by supplying our day-to-day needs and by providing a secure and affluent life for all classes of people.

Molto bene. Intanto, in compagnia dell'industria, la bassezza dell'animo, la freddezza, l'egoismo, l'avarizia, la falsità e la perfidia mercantile, tutte le qualità e le passioni più depravatrici e più indegne dell'uomo incivilito, sono in vigore, e moltiplicano senza fine; ma le virtù si aspettano.

XLV

Gran rimedio della maldicenza, appunto come delle afflizioni d'animo, è il tempo. Se il mondo biasima qualche nostro istituto o andamento, buono o cattivo, a noi non bisogna altro che perseverare. Passato poco tempo, la materia divenendo trita, i maledici l'abbandonano, per cercare delle più recenti. E quanto più fermi ed imperturbati ci mostreremo noi nel seguitar oltre, disprezzando le voci, tanto più presto ciò che fu condannato in principio, o che parve strano, sarà tenuto per ragionevole e per regolare: perchè il mondo, il quale non crede mai che chi non cede abbia il torto, condanna alla fine se, ed assolve noi. Onde avviene, cosa assai nota, che i deboli vivono a volontà del mondo, e i forti a volontà loro.

XLVI

Non fa molto onore, non so s'io dica agli uomini o alla virtù, vedere che in tutte le lingue civili, antiche e moderne, le medesime voci significano bontà e sciocchezza, uomo da bene e uomo da poco. Parecchie di questo genere, come in italiano dabbenaggine, in greco εὐήθης, εὐήθεια, prive del significato proprio, nel quale forse sarebbero poco utili, non ritengono, o non ebbero dal principio, altro che il secondo. Tanta stima della bontà è stata fatta in ogni tempo dalla moltitudine; i giudizi della quale, e gl'intimi sentimenti, si manifestano, anche mal gra

Fine. In the meantime, as industry prospers and proliferates, so do certain other things, such as moral depravity, coldness, egoism, greed, falsehood, mercantile treachery, and all the other most ignoble qualities and passions of civilized men— though we expect virtue.

XLV

The great cure for slander, as for afflictions of the soul, is time. If men criticize our institutions or actions, whether good or bad, all we need do is persevere. After a while, once the subject matter becomes stale, the scandalmongers will let it go and look for other, more recent material. And the more resolute and unshakable we are in pursuing a course of action, and the more we disdain critical remarks, the sooner the thing that at first was condemned or seemed strange will come to be accepted as something reasonable and normal. Since the world never faults a man who refuses to yield, in the end it absolves us and condemns itself. Thus it is generally recognized that weak men live in obedience to the world's will, while the strong obey only their own.

XLVI

Surely it's a poor reflection on men or on human virtue—I can't decide which—that in all civilized languages, ancient and modern, the same words signify both goodness and foolishness, both a well-intentioned and a small-minded man. Several words of this sort—such as *dabbenaggine* in Italian and in Greek εὐήθης and εὐήθεια[15]—have lost their primary meaning (which probably made the words rather useless) and now retain only their secondary meaning, which may be the only real meaning they ever had. In every age, the masses have praised goodness and have manifested their attitudes and intimate feelings—if at

do talvolta di lei medesima, nelle forme del linguaggio. Costante giudizio della moltitudine, non meno che, contraddicendo al linguaggio il discorso, costantemente dissimulato, è, che nessuno che possa eleggere, elegga di esser buono: gli sciocchi sieno buoni, perchè altro non possono.

XLVII

L'uomo è condannato o a consumare la gioventù senza proposito, la quale è il solo tempo di far frutto per l'età che viene, e di provvedere al proprio stato; o a spenderla in procacciare godimenti a quella parte della sua vita, nella quale egli non sarà più atto a godere.

XLVIII

Quanto sia grande l'amore che la natura ci ha dato verso i nostri simili, si può comprendere da quello che fa qualunque animale, e il fanciullo inesperto, se si abbatte a vedere la propria immagine in qualche specchio; che, credendola una creatura simile a se, viene in furore e in ismanie, e cerca ogni via di nuocere a quella creatura e di ammazzarla. Gli uccellini domestici, mansueti come sono per natura e per costume, si spingono contro allo specchio stizzosamente, stridendo, colle ali inarcate e col becco aperto, e lo percuotono; e la scimmia, quando può, lo gitta in terra, e lo stritola co' piedi.

XLIX

Naturalmente l'animale odia il suo simile, e qualora ciò è richiesto all'interesse proprio, l'offende. Perciò l'odio nè le ingiurie degli uomini non si possono fuggire: il disprezzo si può in gran parte. Onde sono il più delle volte poco a proposito gli

times unconsciously—in the forms of language. And their constant attitude, which must be just as constantly disguised since it contradicts their language, is that no one who can choose will choose to be good: let fools be good, since they don't know any better.

XLVII

Man is doomed either to squander his youth, which is the only time he has to store provisions for the coming years and provide for his own well-being, or to spend his youth procuring pleasures in advance for that time of life when he will be too old to enjoy them.

XLVIII

We can understand the great love nature has given us for our own kind by observing what an animal or inexperienced child does when he happens upon his own image in a mirror. Believing the image to be one of his fellow creatures, the animal goes into a fit of frantic rage and tries his best to injure or kill that other creature. Small domestic birds, though docile by nature and habit, peevishly hurl themselves against their mirror; with arched wings and open beak they chirp wildly and thrash at their reflected image. And a monkey, given the opportunity, will throw a mirror to the ground and crush it with his foot.

XLIX

Animals naturally hate their own kind, and they hurt their fellow creatures whenever their own interests are at stake. This is why it's impossible to avoid men's hatred and insults. But one can for the most part avoid men's scorn; therefore, the def-

ossequi che i giovani e le persone nuove nel mondo prestano a
chi viene loro alle mani, non per viltà, nè per altro interesse,
ma per un desiderio benevolo di non incorrere inimicizie e di
guadagnare gli animi. Del qual desiderio non vengono a capo,
e in qualche modo nocciono alla loro estimazione; perchè nell'
ossequiato cresce il concetto di se medesimo, e quello dell'osse-
quioso scema. Chi non cerca dagli uomini utilità o grido, nè anche cerchi amore, che non si ottiene; e, se vuole udire il mio
consiglio, mantenga la propria dignità intera, rendendo non
più che il debito a ciascheduno. Alquanto più odiato e persegui-
tato sarà così che altrimenti, ma non molte volte disprezzato.

L

In un libro che hanno gli Ebrei di sentenze e di detti vari, tra-
dotto, come si dice, d'arabico, o più verisimilmente, secondo
alcuni, di fattura pure ebraica, fra molte altre cose di nessun
rilievo, si legge, che non so qual sapiente, essendogli detto da
uno, io ti vo' bene, rispose: oh perchè no? se non sei nè della
mia religione, nè parente mio, nè vicino, nè persona che mi
mantenga. L'odio verso i propri simili, è maggiore verso i più
simili. I giovani sono, per mille ragioni, più atti all'amicizia che
gli altri. Nondimeno è quasi impossibile un'amicizia durevole
tra due che menino parimente vita giovanile; dico quella sorte
di vita che si chiama così oggi, cioè dedita principalmente alle
donne. Anzi tra questi tali è meno possibile che mai, sì per la
veemenza delle passioni, sì per le rivalità in amore e le gelosie
che nascono tra essi inevitabilmente, e perchè, come è notato
da Madama di Staël, gli altrui successi prosperi colle donne
sempre fanno dispiacere, anche al maggiore amico del fortunato. Le donne sono, dopo i danari, quella cosa in cui la

erence young men and inexperienced people show toward
chance acquaintances is usually wasteful. They defer not from
cowardice or some other interest, but rather because they sincerely wish to avoid enmity and to win over the hearts of others. But this desire does not come to very much, indeed in
some ways it undermines self-esteem, for such deference diminishes one's own self-respect while increasing that of the
person deferred to. One who asks neither usefulness nor acclaim from other men should not seek their love, which is not
to be had. If he cares to follow my advice, let him give others
only what he owes them, sacrificing none of his own dignity.
He may then be a bit more hated and persecuted, but he will
seldom be scorned.

L

The Hebrews have a book of maxims and aphorisms said to
be either a translation from Arabic or, according to some, more
likely of Hebrew origin. Among many other unimportant
things, it tells of some wise man who, when someone said "I
love you" to him, replied: "Well, why not? You're not of my re-
ligion, not my neighbor, not my relative, and not my patron." [16]
Hatred for one's own kind is greatest toward those closest to
us. For any number of reasons, young men are better suited for
friendship than anyone else. Yet lasting friendship is practically impossible between two men who lead similarly "youthful" lives. I mean the kind of life that goes by that name today,
a life dedicated primarily to women. The vehement passions,
amorous rivalries, and jealousy that inevitably come between
such men make lasting friendship all the more impossible. For
as Madame de Staël has noted, the success *someone else* enjoys
with a woman is bound to make other men unhappy, even the
fortunate man's best friend. [17] Women are second only to mon-

gente è meno trattabile e meno capace di accordi, e dove i conoscenti, gli amici, i fratelli cangiano l'aspetto e la natura loro
ordinaria: perchè gli uomini sono amici e parenti, anzi sono civili e uomini, non fino agli altari, giusta il proverbio antico, ma
fino ai danari e alle donne: quivi diventano selvaggi e bestie. E
nelle cose donnesche, se è minore l'inumanità, l'invidia è maggiore che nei danari: perchè in quelle ha più interesse la vanità;
ovvero, per dir meglio, perchè v'ha interesse un amor proprio,
che fra tutti è il più proprio e il più delicato. E benchè ognuno
nelle occasioni faccia altrettanto, mai non si vede alcuno sorridere o dire parole dolci a una donna, che tutti i presenti non
si sforzino, o di fuori o fra se medesimi, di metterlo amara-
mente in derisione. Onde, quantunque la metà del piacere dei
successi prosperi in questo genere, come anche per lo più negli
altri, consista in raccontarli, è al tutto fuori di luogo il conferire
che i giovani fanno le loro gioie amorose, massime con altri
giovani: perchè nessun ragionamento fu mai ad alcuno più
rincrescevole; e spessissime volte, anche narrando il vero, sono
scherniti.

LI

Vedendo quanto poche volte gli uomini nelle loro azioni
sono guidati da un giudizio retto di quello che può loro giovare
o nuocere, si conosce quanto facilmente debba trovarsi ingannato chi proponendosi d'indovinare alcuna risoluzione occul-
ta, esamina sottilmente in che sia posta la maggiore utilità di
colui o di coloro a cui tale risoluzione si aspetta. Dice il Guicciardini nel principio del decimosettimo libro, parlando dei discorsi fatti in proposito di partiti che prenderebbe Francesco
primo, re di Francia, dopo la sua liberazione dalla fortezza di

ey in making people intractable and disagreeable; it's here that
acquaintances, friends, and brothers alter their appearance and
change their everyday nature. For men remain friends and rel-
atives—indeed, they remain civilized and human—not "unto
the altars of worship," as the ancient proverb says, but only
"unto" money and women, at which point they turn into beasts
and savages. And although there is less inhumanity involved
in affairs with women than in money matters, the envy involved is greater because with women vanity plays a larger
part. Or rather, I should say it's because self-love is involved,
this being more personal and fragile than anything else. It's impossible for a man to smile or speak sweet words to a woman—
though, given the opportunity, all men do so—without being
bitterly ridiculed sooner or later by all those present. And so,
however much we enjoy telling others about our successes
with women—here, as in most things, our delight lies in the
telling—it's completely out of place for a young man to confide
his love affairs to others, most of all to other young men. This
is absolutely the last kind of conversation anyone wants to
hear; most of the time such men are ridiculed, even when telling the truth.

LI

We know that men seldom act from a correct sense of what
may be harmful or useful to them. One is therefore easily deceived when he tries to anticipate some undisclosed decision,
studiously examining how best to exploit the person or persons expected to make the decision. At the beginning of Book
17 of *The History of Italy*, Guicciardini comments on the argu-
ments over which side Francis I, King of France, would take
after his release from the Madrid fortress: "Those who quar-
reled in this way perhaps thought more about what the king

Madrid: "considerarono forse quegli che discorsero in questo modo, più quello che ragionevolmente doveva fare, che non considerarono quale sia la natura e la prudenza dei Franzesi; errore nel quale certamente spesso si cade nelle consulte e nei giudizi che si fanno della disposizione e volontà di altri." Il Guicciardini è forse il solo storico tra i moderni, che abbia e conosciuti molto gli uomini, e filosofato circa gli avvenimenti attenendosi alla cognizione della natura umana, e non piuttosto a una certa scienza politica, separata dalla scienza dell' uomo, e per lo più chimerica, della quale si sono serviti comunemente quegli storici, massime oltramontani ed oltramarini, che hanno voluto pur discorrere intorno ai fatti, non contentandosi, come la maggior parte, di narrarli per ordine, senza pensare più avanti.

LII

Nessuno si creda avere imparato a vivere, se non ha imparato a tenere per un purissimo suono di sillabe le profferte che gli sono fatte da chicchessia, e più le più spontanee, per solenni e per ripetute che possano essere: nè solo le profferte, ma le istanze vivissime ed infinite che molti fanno acciocchè altri si prevalga delle facoltà loro; e specificano i modi e le circostanze della cosa, e con ragioni rimuovono le difficoltà. Che se alla fine, o persuaso, o forse vinto dal tedio di sì fatte istanze, o per qualunque causa, tu ti conduci a scoprire ad alcuno di questi tali qualche tuo bisogno, tu vedi colui subito impallidire, poi mutato discorso, o risposto parole di nessun rilievo, lasciarti senza conchiusione; e da indi innanzi, per lungo tempo, non sarà piccola fortuna se, con molta fatica, ti verrà fatto di rivederlo, o se, ricordandotegli per iscritto, ti sarà risposto. Gli uomini non vogliono beneficare, e per la molestia della cosa in se, e perchè i bisogni e le sventure dei conoscenti non mancano

could reasonably be expected to do, instead of considering the true nature and discretion of the French. One is often apt to fall into this kind of error when basing one's advice and opinions on the will and disposition of others." Guicciardini is perhaps the only modern historian who not only knew a lot about men, but whose knowledge of human nature also formed the basis of his historical philosophy. He avoided any political science that could be divorced from the knowledge of man (and therefore mostly illusory), although this divided approach is common practice among historians, especially those north of Italy and overseas. Being unsatisfied, like most historians, with merely narrating facts in chronological order, they have sought to discuss the facts without thinking beyond them.

LII

Let no one think he has learned to live until he has first learned to regard the generous gestures people make as nothing more than sheer syllabic noise, all the more when the repetition and seriousness of such offers make them seem spontaneous. I'm speaking not only of offers of assistance, but also of the countless lively propositions by which people make their services available to others. They specify the details and circumstances of your problem, then explain away all the difficulties. But once you have been won over—or simply overwhelmed by the tedious repetition of his proposals—if then you reveal some genuine need to such a person, you will see him suddenly turn pale. He will change the topic of conversation or give you some irrelevant answer, then leave you hanging. Consider yourself lucky if at some future time he tries to see you again or answers your letters. Men refuse to help others not just because it's a nuisance in itself, but also because

di fare a ciascuno qualche piacere; ma amano l'opinione di be-
nefattori, e la gratitudine altrui, e quella superiorità che viene
dal benefizio. Però quello che non vogliono dare, offrono: e
quanto più ti veggono fiero, più insistono, prima per umiliarti
e per farti arrossire, poi perchè tanto meno temono che tu non
accetti le loro offerte. Così con grandissimo coraggio si spingono oltre fino all'ultima estremità, disprezzando il presentis-
simo pericolo di riuscire impostori, con isperanza di non essere
mai altro che ringraziati; finchè alla prima voce che significhi
domanda, si pongono in fuga.

LIII

Diceva Bione, filosofo antico: è impossibile piacere alla moltitudine, se non diventando un pasticcio, o del vino dolce. Ma
questo impossibile, durando lo stato sociale degli uomini, sarà
cercato sempre, anco da chi dica, ed anco da chi talvolta creda
di non cercarlo: come, durante la nostra specie, i più conoscenti della condizione umana, persevereranno fino alla morte
cercando felicità, e promettendosene.

LIV

Abbiasi per assioma generale che, salvo per tempo corto,
l'uomo, non ostante qualunque certezza ed evidenza delle cose
contrarie, non lascia mai tra se e se, ed anche nascondendo ciò
a tutti gli altri, di creder vere quelle cose, la credenza delle quali
gli è necessaria alla tranquillità dell'animo, e, per dir così, a
poter vivere. Il vecchio, massime se egli usa nel mondo, mai
fino all'estremo non lascia di credere nel segreto della sua

everyone in some way enjoys seeing his acquaintances in need.
Men, however, like to be thought of as benefactors. They enjoy
the gratitude of others and the feeling of superiority that comes
from doing good. But they really have no intention of giving
what they offer; and the more proudly you act, the more they
insist, at first in order to humiliate and embarrass you and then
because they are much less afraid that you will accept their offer. Their extraordinary bravery thus drives them to the far-
thest extremes. They are contemptuous of the constant danger
of being exposed as impostors and ask in return nothing more
than the gratitude of others. But as soon as the first real question is raised, they turn and run.

LIII

The ancient philosopher Bion said that it's impossible to
please the masses unless you turn yourself into sweet wine
and cake. But certain people will always seek to achieve this
"impossibility" for as long as the social state lasts, even those
who say—and who sometimes even believe—that they are not
seeking it. Likewise, as long as our species lasts, those most
familiar with the human condition will persist till death searching for, and promising themselves, happiness.

LIV

Let us set down a working assumption: except for short periods, and despite all the contradictory evidence, man never
stops believing that certain things are true. He clings to such
beliefs—privately, without letting on to anyone else—whenever they are essential to his peace of mind or when they en-
able him, so to speak, to go on living. An old man, especially if
he is publicly active, will hold out till the very end secretly be-

mente, benchè ad ogni occasione protesti il contrario, di potere, per un'eccezione singolarissima dalla regola universale, in qualche modo ignoto e inesplicabile a lui medesimo, fare ancora un poco d'impressione alle donne: perchè il suo stato sarebbe troppo misero, se egli fosse persuaso compiutamente di essere escluso in tutto e per sempre da quel bene in cui finalmente l'uomo civile, ora a un modo ora a un altro, e quando più quando meno aggirandosi, viene a riporre l'utilità della vita. La donna licenziosa, benchè vegga tutto giorno mille segni dell'opinione pubblica intorno a sè, crede costantemente di essere tenuta dalla generalità per donna onesta; e che solo un piccolo numero di suoi confidenti antichi e nuovi (dico piccolo a respetto del pubblico) sappiano, e tengano celato al mondo, ed anche gli uni di loro agli altri, il vero dell'esser suo. L'uomo di portamenti vili, e, per la stessa sua viltà e per poco ardire, sollecito dei giudizi altrui, crede che le sue azioni sieno interpretate nel miglior modo, e che i veri motivi di esse non sieno compresi. Similmente nelle cose materiali, il Buffon osserva che il malato in punto di morte non dà vera fede nè a medici nè ad amici, ma solo all'intima sua speranza, che gli promette scampo dal pericolo presente. Lascio la stupenda credulità e incredulità de' mariti circa le mogli, materia di novelle, di scene, di motteggi e di riso eterno a quelle nazioni appresso le quali il matrimonio è irrevocabile. E così discorrendo, non è cosa al mondo tanto falsa nè tanto assurda, che non sia tenuta vera dagli uomini più sensati, ogni volta che l'animo non trova modo di accomodarsi alla cosa contraria, e di darsene pace. Non tralascerò che i vecchi sono meno disposti che i giovani a rimuoversi dal credere ciò che fa per loro, e ad abbracciare quelle credenze che gli offendono: perchè i giovani hanno più animo di levare gli occhi incontro ai mali, e più attitudine o a sostenerne la coscienza o a perirne.

lieving (though always claiming just the opposite) that by some absolutely singular exception to the universal rule, and in a way unknown and inexplicable even to himself, he can still make a bit of an impression on women. For it would cause him too much grief to think himself totally and forever denied this particular pleasure, one in which civilized man somehow manages—usually by fooling himself in some way—to place the value of his life. A woman of easy virtue may *see* what the public thinks of her yet firmly believe that most people think her an honest and well-behaved woman. She thinks that only a few of her old and new confidants (few, that is, with respect to the general public) know what she is really like, and that they keep the truth hidden not just from the world but from each other. A man who lives a cowardly life and whose cowardice and timidity make him solicitous of other people's opinions believes that his actions are interpreted in the best light and that people cannot see the real motives behind them. Likewise, in material things, Buffon notes that a dying man never trusts his doctor or friends, but trusts only in silent hope, in the secret promise of escape from his present danger.[18] I will not even mention the extraordinary credulity and incredulity of husbands toward their wives, the subject of novels, plays, general banter, and eternal laughter in countries where marriage is irrevocable. So we see that there is nothing in the world so false or absurd that it will not be taken as truth even by the most sensible person whenever his mind fails to accommodate or find peace in some contrary notion. I must also say that the aged are less inclined than young people to disbelieve things that work in their favor, and less inclined to embrace beliefs that hurt them; for the young are more willing to face trouble directly and are better prepared either to bear the knowledge of evil or to perish from it.

LV

Una donna è derisa se piange di vero cuore il marito morto, ma biasimata altamente se, per qualunque grave ragione o necessità, comparisce in pubblico, o smette il bruno, un giorno prima dell'uso. È assioma trito, ma non perfetto, che il mondo si contenta dell'apparenza. Aggiungasi per farlo compiuto, che il mondo non si contenta mai, e spesso non si cura, e spesso è intollerantissimo della sostanza. Quell'antico si studiava più d'esser uomo da bene che di parere; ma il mondo ordina di parere uomo da bene, e di non essere.

LVI

La schiettezza allora può giovare, quando è usata ad arte, o quando, per la sua rarità, non l'è data fede.

LVII

Gli uomini si vergognano, non delle ingiurie che fanno, ma di quelle che ricevono. Però ad ottenere che gl'ingiuriatori si vergognino, non v'è altra via, che di rendere loro il cambio.

LVIII

I timidi non hanno meno amor proprio che gli arroganti; anzi più, o vogliamo dire più sensitivo; e perciò temono: e si guardano di non pungere gli altri, non per istima che ne facciano maggiore che gl'insolenti e gli arditi, ma per evitare d'esser punti essi, atteso l'estremo dolore che ricevono da ogni puntura.

LV

A woman is ridiculed if she sincerely mourns the death of her husband; but if for some serious reason or need she appears in public or ceases to mourn even one day sooner than custom allows, she is severely criticized. It is a commonplace but flawed axiom that the world is satisfied by appearances. To complete this, let us add that the world is never satisfied by *substance*: it does not care much about substance and often absolutely refuses to tolerate it. The ancients tried to *be* good men, rather than merely seem good—but the world demands that a man seem, not be, good.

LVI

Pure sincerity, then, has a practical value when used as artifice or when, because of its rarity, it is not trusted.

LVII

Men are shamed by the insults they receive, not by those they inflict. So the only way to shame people who insult us is to pay them back in kind.

LVIII

The timid possess no less self-love than the arrogant; indeed, they possess more. Or rather we should say they are more sensitive and hence feel fear. They are careful not to hurt others not because they have more respect for aggressive, insolent men, but rather to avoid being hurt in return—the pain, they know, drives deep.

LIX

È cosa detta più volte, che quanto decrescono negli stati le virtù solide, tanto crescono le apparenti. Pare che le lettere sieno soggette allo stesso fato, vedendo come, al tempo nostro, più che va mancando, non posso dire l'uso, ma la memoria delle virtù dello stile, più cresce il nitore delle stampe. Nessun libro classico fu stampato in altri tempi con quella eleganza che oggi si stampano le gazzette, e l'altre ciance politiche, fatte per durare un giorno: ma dell'arte dello scrivere non si conosce più nè s'intende appena il nome. E credo che ogni uomo da bene, all'aprire o leggere un libro moderno, senta pietà di quelle carte e di quelle forme di caratteri così terse, adoperate a rappresentar parole sì orride, e pensieri la più parte sì scioperati.

LX

Dice il La Bruyère una cosa verissima; che è più facile ad un libro mediocre di acquistar grido per virtù di una riputazione già ottenuta dall'autore, che ad un autore di venire in riputazione per mezzo di un libro eccellente. A questo si può soggiungere, che la via forse più diritta di acquistar fama, è di affermare con sicurezza e pertinacia, e in quanti più modi è possibile, di averla acquistata.

LXI

Uscendo della gioventù, l'uomo resta privato della proprietà di comunicare e, per dir così, d'ispirare colla presenza se agli altri; e perdendo quella specie d'influsso che il giovane manda ne' circostanti, e che congiunge questi a lui, e fa che sentano verso lui sempre qualche sorte d'inclinazione, conosce, non senza un dolore nuovo, di trovarsi nelle compagnie come di-

LIX

It has often been said that the faster genuine virtues decline, the faster apparent virtues spring up. Literature is evidently subject to the same fate, for in our own age the more the memory (I cannot say the *practice*) of fine writing fades away, the more the splendors of publication increase. In past ages, no classical book was ever printed with the elegance that today characterizes pamphlets and other political nonsense made to last no longer than a day. But the art of writing is no longer understood; people do not even know what these words mean. I think that any compassionate man who opens or reads through a modern book must feel a certain pity for those pages, where such clearly defined characters represent such ugly words and express such insipid ideas.

LX

What La Bruyère says is absolutely true: it is easier for an ordinary or mediocre book to win acclaim because of its author's ready-made reputation than it is for an author to make a reputation by writing an excellent book.[19] To this we might add that perhaps the most direct way of acquiring fame is by insisting stubbornly and in as many ways as possible that we have already acquired it.

LXI

As a man grows older, he finds that he no longer has the power to communicate with others or, so to speak, to inspire them with his presence. In losing the kind of influence that young men have on people, which makes others feel a kind of constant communal attraction toward them, he arrives at a new and painful realization: at social gatherings he is isolated from

viso da tutti, e intorniato di creature sensibili poco meno indifferenti verso lui che quelle prive di senso.

LXII

Il primo fondamento dell'essere apparecchiato in giuste occasioni a spendersi, è il molto apprezzarsi.

LXIII

Il concetto che l'artefice ha dell'arte sua o lo scienziato della sua scienza, suol essere grande in proporzione contraria al concetto ch'egli ha del proprio valore nella medesima.

LXIV

Quell'artefice o scienziato o cultore di qualunque disciplina, che sarà usato paragonarsi, non con altri cultori di essa, ma con essa medesima, più che sarà eccellente, più basso concetto avrà di se: perchè meglio conoscendo le profondità di quella, più inferiore si troverà nel paragone. Così quasi tutti gli uomini grandi sono modesti: perchè si paragonano continuamente, non cogli altri, ma con quell'idea del perfetto che hanno dinanzi allo spirito, infinitamente più chiara e maggiore di quella che ha il volgo; e considerano quanto sieno lontani dal conseguirla. Dove che i volgari facilmente, e forse alle volte con verità, si credono avere, non solo conseguita, ma superata quell'idea di perfezione che cape negli animi loro.

everyone else, surrounded by sensitive creatures who are only a little less indifferent toward him than totally insensitive creatures.

LXII

The first rule in preparing to give of oneself at the right times is to hold oneself in high esteem.

LXIII

The artist's conception of his art or the scientist's of his science is usually as great as his conception of his own worth is small.

LXIV

If an artist, scientist, or intellectual of whatever discipline is in the habit of comparing himself not to other members of his discipline but rather to the discipline itself, then the more intelligent he is the lower will be his opinion of himself. For his sense of his own inferiority grows in direct proportion to his deepening knowledge of his discipline. This is why all great men are modest: they consistently measure themselves not in comparison to other people but to the idea of perfection ever present in their minds, an ideal infinitely clearer and greater than any the common people have, and they also realize how far they are from fulfilling their ideal. The masses, on the other hand, readily and perhaps rightly believe that they have not only realized the idea of perfection they have in mind, but that they have surpassed it.

LXV

Nessuna compagnia è piacevole al lungo andare, se non di persone dalle quali importi o piaccia a noi d'essere sempre più stimati. Perciò le donne, volendo che la loro compagnia non cessi di piacere dopo breve tempo, dovrebbero studiare di rendersi tali, che potesse essere desiderata durevolmente la loro stima.

LXVI

Nel secolo presente i neri sono creduti di razza e di origine totalmente diversi da' bianchi, e nondimeno totalmente uguali a questi in quanto è a diritti umani. Nel secolo decimosesto i neri, creduti avere una radice coi bianchi, ed essere una stessa famiglia, fu sostenuto, massimamente da' teologi spagnuoli, che in quanto a diritti, fossero per natura, e per volontà divina, di gran lunga inferiori a noi. E nell'uno e nell'altro secolo i neri furono e sono venduti e comperati, e fatti lavorare in catene sotto la sferza. Tale è l'etica; e tanto le credenze in materia di morale hanno che fare colle azioni.

LXVII

Poco propriamente si dice che la noia è mal comune. Comune è l'essere disoccupato, o sfaccendato per dir meglio; non annoiato. La noia non è se non di quelli in cui lo spirito è qualche cosa. Più può lo spirito in alcuno, più la noia è frequente, penosa e terribile. La massima parte degli uomini trova bastante occupazione in che che sia, e bastante diletto in qualunque occupazione insulsa; e quando è del tutto disoccupata, non prova perciò gran pena. Di qui nasce che gli uomini di sentimento sono sì poco intesi circa la noia, e fanno il volgo talvolta mara-

LXV

We enjoy company over a long period only if we feel happy or gratified that their esteem for us is constantly growing. So, if women want their companionship to remain pleasurable in the long run, they ought to learn to be like this, so that their esteem will be lastingly desired.

LXVI

In the present century, black people are believed to be totally different from whites in race and origin, yet totally equal to them with regard to human rights. In the sixteenth century, when blacks were thought to come from the same roots and to be of the same family as whites, it was held, most of all by Spanish theologians, that with regard to rights blacks were by nature and by Divine Will greatly inferior to us. In both centuries, blacks have been bought and sold and made to work in chains under the whip. Such is ethics; and such is the extent to which moral beliefs have anything to do with actions.

LXVII

It is hardly correct to say that *noia* is a common problem.[20] Idleness—or rather, loafing—is common, not *noia*. *Noia* is felt only by those who possess meaningful spirit. The more spirit a person has, the more frequent, painful, and terrible his sense of *noia* is. Most men are satisfied doing just about anything and are sufficiently happy in any banal occupation; when they are completely idle, then, they feel no great pain. This is why men of genuine feeling who suffer from *noia* are so little understood, and why they sometimes astonish common people—

vigliare e talvolta ridere, quando parlano della medesima e se
ne dolgono con quella gravità di parole, che si usa in proposito
dei mali maggiori e più inevitabili della vita.

LXVIII

La noia è in qualche modo il più sublime dei sentimenti umani. Non che io creda che dall'esame di tale sentimento nasca-
no quelle conseguenze che molti filosofi hanno stimato di rac-
corne, ma nondimeno il non potere essere soddisfatto da
alcuna cosa terrena, nè, per dir così, dalla terra intera; considerare l'ampiezza inestimabile dello spazio, il numero e la mole
maravigliosa dei mondi, e trovare che tutto è poco e piccino alla
capacità dell'animo proprio; immaginarsi il numero dei mondi
infinito, e l'universo infinito, e sentire che l'animo e il desiderio
nostro sarebbe ancora più grande che sì fatto universo; e sempre accusare le cose d'insufficienza e di nullità, e patire mancamento e voto, e però noia, pare a me il maggior segno di grandezza e di nobiltà, che si vegga della natura umana. Perciò la
noia è poco nota agli uomini di nessun momento, e pochissimo
o nulla agli altri animali.

LXIX

Dalla famosa lettera di Cicerone a Lucceio, dove induce
questo a comporre una storia della congiura di Catilina, e da
un'altra lettera meno divulgata e non meno curiosa, in cui Vero
imperatore prega Frontone suo maestro a scrivere, come fu
fatto, la guerra partica amministrata da esso Vero; lettere so-
migliantissime a quelle che oggi si scrivono ai giornalisti, se
non che i moderni domandano articoli di gazzette, e quelli, per
essere antichi, domandavano libri; si può argomentare in qual-

and sometimes provoke their laughter—when they talk and complain about it in the same kind of weighty, serious language usually reserved for life's worst and most inevitable ills.

LXVIII

Noia is in some ways the most sublime of human feelings, though I don't believe it's responsible for bringing about *all* the effects that many philosophers attribute to it. But there is certainly at least one: the inability to be satisfied by any worldly thing or, so to speak, by the entire world. To consider the inestimable amplitude of space, the number of worlds and their astonishing size, then to discover that all this is small and insignificant compared to the capacity of one's own mind; to imagine the infinite number of worlds, the infinite universe, then feel that our mind and aspirations might be even greater than such a universe; to accuse things always of being inadequate and meaningless; to suffer want, emptiness, and hence *noia*—this seems to me the chief sign of the grandeur and nobility of human nature. This is why *noia* is practically unknown to unambitious men and scarcely or not at all known to other animals.

LXIX

Cicero's famous letter to Lucceius, where he persuades Lucceius to write a history of the Cataline conspiracy;[21] and another letter, less well known but no less curious, in which the Emperor Verus asks his teacher Fronto to write about the Parthian War that he, Verus, had waged[22]—both are incredibly similar to letters now written to journalists. Except that the moderns request newspaper articles, while the others, since they were ancients, asked for books. One can quarrel in some small way

che piccola parte di che fede sia la storia, ancora quando è scritta
da uomini contemporanei e di gran credito al loro tempo.

LXX

Moltissimi di quegli errori che si chiamano fanciullaggini, in
cui sogliono cadere i giovani inesperti del mondo, e quelli che,
o giovani o vecchi, sono condannati dalla natura ad essere più
che uomini e parere sempre fanciulli, non consistono, a consi-
derarli bene, se non in questo; che i sopraddetti pensano e si
governano come se gli uomini fossero meno fanciulli di quel
che sono. Certamente quella cosa che prima e forse più di
qualunque altra percuote di maraviglia l'animo de' giovani
bene educati, all'entrare che fanno nel mondo, è la frivolezza
delle occupazioni ordinarie, dei passatempi, dei discorsi, delle
inclinazioni e degli spiriti delle persone: alla qual frivolezza
eglino poi coll'uso a poco a poco si adattano, ma non senza
pena e difficoltà, parendo loro da principio di avere a tornare
un'altra volta fanciulli. E così è veramente; che il giovane di
buona indole e buona disciplina, quando incomincia, come si
dice, a vivere, dee per forza rifarsi indietro, e rimbambire, per
dir così, un poco; e si trova molto ingannato dalla credenza che
aveva, di dovere allora in tutto diventar uomo, e deporre ogni
avanzo di fanciullezza. Perchè al contrario gli uomini in generalità, per quanto procedano negli anni, sempre continuano a
vivere in molta parte fanciullescamente.

LXXI

Dalla sopraddetta opinione che il giovane ha degli uomini,
cioè perchè li crede più uomini che non sono, nasce che si sgo-
menta ad ogni suo fallo, e si pensa aver perduta la stima di
quelli che ne furono spettatori o consapevoli. Poi di là a poco si

about how trustworthy history is, especially when written by
contemporaries highly regarded in their own time.

LXX

A vast number of those mistakes that we call "childish" are
made not only by young people who have little worldly experience but also by those, young or old, who are doomed by nature to be something more than men yet seem eternal children.
Such errors, if we look carefully, are due to one thing: all those
mentioned above think and behave as if men were less childish
than they really are. Surely the first and perhaps most conspic-
uous thing that shocks and astonishes young well-educated
men when they enter public life is the frivolousness of the
ordinary occupations, pastimes, conversations, inclinations,
and spirit of people. A frivolousness that they slowly get accustomed to with experience, but not without the pain and difficulty of adjusting to what seems to be a second childhood. It's
true, therefore, that when a young man of good character and
sound discipline begins, as they say, to really live, he must necessarily regress and become something of a child again. And
he feels very much deceived by what he once believed—that
he had to be a man in all things and had to put away all the
remnants of childhood. For, on the contrary, as men get older
they continue to live more or less childishly.

LXXI

From the abovementioned opinion that a young man has of
people—that he thinks them more grown-up than they really
are—it's natural for him to feel upset over every little mistake
he makes, since he thinks he has lost the respect of those who

riconforta, non senza maraviglia, vedendosi trattare da quei medesimi coi modi di prima. Ma gli uomini non sono sì pronti a disistimare, perchè non avrebbero mai a far altro, e dimenticano gli errori, perchè troppi ne veggono e ne commettono di continuo. Nè sono sì consentanei a se stessi, che non ammirino facilmente oggi chi forse derisero ieri. Ed è manifesto quanto spesso da noi medesimi sia biasimata, anche con parole assai gravi, o messa in burla questa o quella persona assente, nè perciò privata in maniera alcuna della nostra stima, o trattata poi, quando è presente, con altri modi che innanzi.

LXXII

Come il giovane è ingannato dal timore in questo, così sono ingannati dalla loro speranza quelli che avvedendosi di essere o caduti o abbassati nella stima d'alcuno, tentano di rilevarsi a forza di uffici e di compiacenze che fanno a quello. La stima non è prezzo di ossequi: oltre che essa, non diversa in ciò dall'amicizia, è come un fiore, che pesto una volta gravemente, o appassito, mai più non ritorna. Però da queste che possiamo dire umiliazioni, non si raccoglie altro frutto che di essere più disistimato. Vero è che il disprezzo, anche ingiusto, di chicchessia è sì penoso a tollerare, che veggendosene tocchi, pochi sono sì forti che restino immobili, e non si dieno con vari mezzi, per lo più inutilissimi, a cercare di liberarsene. Ed è vezzo assai comune degli uomini mediocri, di usare alterigia e disdegno cogl'indifferenti e con chi mostra curarsi di loro, e ad un segno o ad un sospetto che abbiano di noncuranza, divenire umili per non soffrirla, e spesso ricorrere ad atti vili. Ma anche per questa ragione il partito da prendere se alcuno mostra disprezzarti, è di ricambiarlo con segni di altrettanto disprezzo o maggiore: perchè, secondo ogni verisimiglianza, tu vedrai l'or-

witnessed or heard about his mistake. Then a little later he
feels reassured, and a trifle astonished, to see those same people treat him exactly as they did before. Men, however, are not
so quick to disesteem others, since it would claim all their time;
and they forget mistakes because they themselves constantly
see and make so many. Nor are they so consistent that they
will not readily admire someone today whom yesterday they
ridiculed. And it's obvious how often we ourselves cast blame
on this or that absent person, sometimes in very strong language, or make jokes about him. But this is not to deprive him
in any way of our respect, nor does it mean that we will treat
him in his presence any differently than before.

LXXII

As fear of disrespect deceives a young man, so does hope deceive those who try to win back lost or faded esteem with services and amenities. Esteem, however, cannot be bought with
deference; furthermore, it is no different from friendship in
that, like a flower, if it wilts or is crushed just once, it can never
again come back to life. And so the only fruit to be harvested
from these actions—call them *humiliations*—is greater disesteem. True, a person's contempt is so painful to endure that
once it strikes, even if unjustified, few are strong enough to remain unshaken or to resist trying to get free of it by various
and frequently useless means. Mediocre men are very commonly arrogant and contemptuous toward passive men as well
as toward their sympathisers; and yet, at the first sign or hint
of unconcern, these same men will become humble so as not to
suffer such indifference, and often they resort to cowardly actions. For this very reason, the thing to do when someone
shows disdain for you is to act the same way in return, showing him equal or even greater disdain; in all likelihood you will

goglio di quello cangiarsi in umiltà. Ed in ogni modo non può mancare che quegli non senta dentro tale offensione, e al tempo medesimo tale stima di te, che sieno abbastanza a punirlo.

LXXIII

Come le donne quasi tutte, così ancora gli uomini assai comunemente, e più i più superbi, si cattivano e si conservano colla noncuranza e col disprezzo, ovvero, al bisogno, con dimostrare fintamente di non curarli e di non avere stima di loro. Perchè quella stessa superbia onde un numero infinito d'uomini usa alterigia cogli umili e con tutti quelli che gli fanno segno d'onore, rende lui curante e sollecito e bisognoso della stima e degli sguardi di quelli che non lo curano, o che mostrano non badargli. Donde nasce non di rado, anzi spesso, nè solamente in amore, una lepida alternativa tra due persone, o l'una o l'altra, con vicenda perpetua, oggi curata e non curante, domani curante e non curata. Anzi si può dire che simile giuoco ed alternativa apparisce in qualche modo, più o manco, in tutta la società umana; e che ogni parte della vita è piena di genti che mirate non mirano, che salutate non rispondono, che seguitate fuggono, e che voltando loro le spalle, o torcendo il viso, si volgono, e s'inchinano, e corrono dietro ad altrui.

LXXIV

Verso gli uomini grandi, e specialmente verso quelli in cui risplende una straordinaria virilità, il mondo è come donna. Non gli ammira solo, ma gli ama: perchè quella loro forza l'innamora. Spesso, come nelle donne, l'amore verso questi tali è maggiore per conto ed in proporzione del disprezzo che essi mostrano, dei mali trattamenti che fanno, e dello stesso timore che ispirano agli uomini. Così Napoleone fu amatissimo dalla Francia, ed oggetto, per dir così, di culto ai soldati, che egli

then see his pride change to humility. In any event, it's certain that the insult he feels inside, together with the respect he has for you, will be sufficient punishment.

LXXIII

Like almost all women, men too, proud men most of all, are very commonly won over—and remain won over—by indifference or disdain, or, if necessary, by pretending neither to respect or care about them. For a man whose pride impels him to act arrogantly toward modest men and those who honor modesty will also, out of pride, be mindful, solicitous, and needful of the esteem and attention of those who ignore or act indifferently toward him. And so not infrequently, indeed often, this results in an amusing predictable turnabout between two people (not limited to love relationships) played out by one or the other: today uncaring but cared for, tomorrow uncared for but caring. In fact, the same kind of reversal game appears in some form in all human society; for every sector of life is filled with people who are admired but do not admire, who when greeted do not reply, who when followed flee, and who will ignore or sneer at one person, then turn, bow, and chase after someone else.

LXXIV

Toward great men, and especially toward those who glow with extraordinary virility, the world is like a woman. She does not just admire them, she *loves* them and is charmed by the special power they possess. The world's love of such men, like a woman's love, often increases in proportion to and by virtue of the contempt they feel for men generally, their wicked treatment of them, and the fear they instill in them. Thus Napoleon was greatly loved by France and was a kind of idol to the very

chiamò carne da cannone, e trattò come tali. Così tanti capitani
che fecero degli uomini simile giudizio ed uso, furono carissimi
ai loro eserciti in vita, ed oggi nelle storie fanno invaghire di se
i lettori. Anche una sorte di brutalità e di stravaganza piace non
poco in questi tali, come alle donne negli amanti. Però Achille è
perfettamente amabile: laddove la bontà di Enea e di Goffredo,
e la saviezza di questi medesimi e di Ulisse, generano quasi
odio.

LXXV

In più altri modi la donna è come una figura di quello che è il
mondo generalmente: perchè la debolezza è proprietà del maggior numero degli uomini; ed essa, verso i pochi forti o di
mente o di cuore o di mano, rende le moltitudini tali, quali
sogliono essere le femmine verso i maschi. Perciò quasi colle
stesse arti si acquistano le donne e il genere umano: con ardire
misto di dolcezza, con tollerare le ripulse, con perseverare fermamente e senza vergogna, si viene a capo, come delle donne,
così dei potenti, dei ricchi, dei più degli uomini in particolare,
delle nazioni e dei secoli. Come colle donne abbattere i rivali, e
far solitudine dintorno a se, così nel mondo è necessario atter-
rare gli emuli e i compagni, e farsi via su pei loro corpi: e si
abbattono questi e i rivali colle stesse armi; delle quali due sono
principalissime, la calunnia e il riso. Colle donne e cogli uomini
riesce sempre a nulla, o certo è malissimo fortunato, chi gli
ama d'amore non finto e non tepido, e chi antepone gl'interessi
loro ai propri. E il mondo è, come le donne, di chi lo seduce,
gode di lui, e lo calpesta.

soldiers he called cannon fodder and whom he treated as such.
Thus so many captains who judged and used men in a similar
way were in their own day dear to their armies and today
charm readers of history. And there's a kind of brutality and
extravagance in such men that people like—the kind women
find appealing in their lovers. Hence Achilles is perfectly lov-
able, whereas the goodness and wisdom of Aeneas and God-
frey, and the wisdom of Ulysses, inspire near hatred.

LXXV

There are other ways in which a woman is a kind of symbol
of the world in general. Most men are weak, and the masses
therefore act toward those few who are strong of mind, heart,
or hand in the same way females usually act toward males.
Women and mankind in general are therefore won over by almost the same devices. By blending courage with gentleness,
by tolerating refusals, and by persevering diligently and un-
ashamedly, a man succeeds quite well with women, succeeds
likewise with rich and powerful men, with almost all men individually, with nations, and with entire ages. Just as it's necessary to get one's rivals out of the way and go it alone with
women, so too in the world it's necessary to knock down your
competitors and companions, making your way up and over
their fallen bodies. Ambitious men and rival lovers both use
the same weapons to wipe out the competition, the chief of
these being slander and laughter. He who loves with a love
that is neither false nor tepid, and who puts the interests of
others before his own, is bound to fail with women and men
alike, or is at least bound to suffer terrible misfortune. The
world, like women, belongs to the man who seduces, enjoys,
and tramples over it.

LXXVI

Nulla è più raro al mondo, che una persona abitualmente sopportabile.

LXXVII

La sanità del corpo è riputata universalmente come ultimo dei beni, e pochi sono nella vita gli atti e le faccende importanti, dove la considerazione della sanità, se vi ha luogo, non sia proposta a qualunque altra. La cagione può essere in parte, ma non però in tutto, che la vita è principalmente dei sani, i quali, come sempre accade, o disprezzano o non credono poter perdere ciò che posseggono. Per recare un esempio fra mille, diversissime cause fanno e che un luogo è scelto a fondarvi una città, e che una città cresce di abitatori; ma tra queste cause non si troverà forse mai la salubrità del sito. Per lo contrario non v'è sito in sulla terra tanto insalubre e tristo, nel quale, indotti da qualche opportunità, gli uomini non si acconcino di buon grado a stare. Spesso un luogo saluberrimo e disabitato è in prossimità di uno poco sano e abitatissimo: e si veggono continuamente le popolazioni abbandonare città e climi salutari, per concorrere sotto cieli aspri, e in luoghi non di rado malsani, e talora mezzo pestilenti, dove sono invitate da altre comoditá. Londra, Madrid e simili, sono città di condizioni pessime alla salute, le quali, per essere capitali, tutto giorno crescono della gente che lascia le abitazioni sanissime delle province. E senza muoverci de' paesi nostri, in Toscana Livorno, a causa del suo commercio, da indi in qua che fu cominciato a popolare, è cresciuto costantemente d'uomini, e cresce sempre; e in sulle porte di Livorno, Pisa, luogo salutevole, e famoso per aria tem-

LXXVI

Nothing in the world is so rare as a person one can always put up with.

LXXVII

Physical health is universally regarded as the ultimate good, and there are few important matters in life where consideration for one's health, if it enters in, does not take precedence over everything else. The reason may be in part, though not entirely, that life belongs mainly to the healthy, who inevitably either disdain it or else feel they can never lose what they already possess. To cite one example among thousands, there are a great many reasons why a place is chosen for founding a city and why a city's population increases, but you probably won't find the wholesomeness of the site listed among the reasons. On the contrary, there is no place on earth so wretched and unhealthy that men, when induced by certain opportunities, are unwilling to adapt themselves to living there. Often a very healthy uninhabited place lies close to another that is very *un*healthy yet heavily populated; time and again people abandon healthy cities and climates in order to converge beneath harsh skies in places that are unhealthy and sometimes half ridden with pestilence, where they are attracted by other conveniences. The conditions in cities like London and Madrid are wretched, but since they are capitals, they swell more each day with people who have left behind the extremely healthy environs of the provinces. We need not look beyond our own borders: the population of Tuscan Leghorn has grown steadily because of its commerce ever since it was first settled, and its numbers continue to grow. And farther inland, Pisa, famous for its temperate balmy air and filled with people when it was

peratissima e soave, già piena di popolo, quando era città navi-
gatrice e potente, è ridotta quasi un deserto, e segue perdendo
ogni giorno più.

LXXVIII

Due o più persone in un luogo pubblico o in un'adunanza
qualsivoglia, che stieno ridendo tra loro in modo osservabile,
nè sappiano gli altri di che, generano in tutti i presenti tale ap-
prensione, che ogni discorso tra questi divien serio, molti am-
mutoliscono, alcuni si partono, i più intrepidi si accostano a
quelli che ridono, procurando di essere accettati a ridere in
compagnia loro. Come se si udissero scoppi di artiglierie vici-
ne, dove fossero genti al buio: tutti n'andrebbero in iscom-
piglio, non sapendo ove potessero toccare i colpi in caso che
l'artiglieria fosse carica a palla. Il ridere concilia stima e rispetto
anche dagl'ignoti, tira a se l'attenzione di tutti i circostanti, e dà
fra questi una sorte di superiorità. E se, come accade, tu ti
ritrovassi in qualche luogo alle volte o non curato, o trattato con
alterigia o scortesemente, tu non hai a far altro che scegliere tra
i presenti uno che ti paia a proposito, e con quello ridere franco
e aperto e con perseveranza, mostrando più che puoi che il riso
ti venga dal cuore: e se forse vi sono alcuni che ti deridano,
ridere con voce più chiara e con più costanza che i derisori. Tu
devi essere assai sfortunato se, avvedutisi del tuo ridere, i più
orgogliosi e i più petulanti della compagnia, e quelli che più
torcevano da te il viso, fatta brevissima resistenza, o non si
danno alla fuga, o non vengono spontanei a chieder pace,
ricercando la tua favella, e forse profferendotisi per amici.
Grande tra gli uomini e di gran terrore è la potenza del riso:
contro il quale nessuno nella sua coscienza trova se munito da
ogni parte. Chi ha coraggio di ridere, è padrone del mondo,
poco altrimenti di chi è preparato a morire.

a powerful maritime city, has become almost a wasteland and declines with each passing day.

LXXVIII

Two or more people laughing openly among themselves in a public place or at a gathering of some sort cause great apprehension in those who do not know what the laughter is about. Their conversations suddenly become serious. Many are struck dumb, some simply leave, while the most fearless ones join in the laughter, hoping thereby to gain acceptance into the group. It's as if people gathered in darkness heard artillery bursts nearby; not knowing where the loaded rounds might land, everybody scatters. Laughter wins esteem and respect even from strangers; it draws the attention of all those present and assumes a kind of superiority. If in company you should find yourself at times either ignored or treated discourteously or condescendingly, all you need do is choose from those present someone suitable and laugh with him openly, frankly, and unstintingly, showing as best you can that your laughter is heartfelt. And if anyone ridicules you, you need only laugh more brightly and diligently than he. Consider yourself truly unlucky if the most haughty and petulant members of the group, and those who sneer at you the most, do not then try to leave, after offering brief resistance, or if they do not come and make peace with you voluntarily, anxious for your conversation and, perhaps, your friendship. The power of laughter among men is great and terrifying, and no one can consciously protect himself entirely from it. He who has the courage to laugh is master of the world and is not much different from one who is prepared to die.

LXXIX

Il giovane non acquista mai l'arte del vivere, non ha, si può dire, un successo prospero nella società, e non prova nell'uso di quella alcun piacere, finchè dura in lui la veemenza dei desiderii. Più ch'egli raffredda, più diventa abile a trattare gli uomini e se stesso. La natura, benignamente come suole, ha ordinato che l'uomo non impari a vivere se non a proporzione che le cause di vivere gli s'involano; non sappia le vie di venire a' suoi fini se non cessato che ha di apprezzarli come felicità celesti, e quando l'ottenerli non gli può arrecare allegrezza più che mediocre; non goda se non divenuto incapace di godimenti vili. Molti si trovano assai giovani di tempo in questo stato ch'io dico; e riescono non di rado bene, perchè desiderano leggermente; essendo nei loro animi anticipata da un concorso di esperienza e d'ingegno, l'età virile. Altri non giungono al detto stato mai nella vita loro: e sono quei pochi in cui la forza de' sentimenti è sì grande in principio, che per corso d'anni non vien meno: i quali più che tutti gli altri godrebbero nella vita, se la natura avesse destinata la vita a godere. Questi per lo contrario sono infelicissimi, e bambini fino alla morte nell'uso del mondo, che non possono apprendere.

LXXX

Rivedendo in capo di qualche anno una persona ch'io avessi conosciuta giovane, sempre alla prima giunta mi è paruto vedere uno che avesse sofferto qualche grande sventura. L'aspetto della gioia e della confidenza non è proprio che della prima età: e il sentimento di ciò che si va perdendo, e delle incomodità corporali che crescono di giorno in giorno, viene generando anche nei più frivoli o più di natura allegra, ed anco

LXXIX

A young man can never learn the art of living, never as it were have any real success in society or enjoy being a part of it, as long as desire burns in him. The more he cools, the more able he is to deal with men and with himself. Nature has ordained, benignly as usual, that man learn to live only in so far as his reasons for living disappear; that he know how to reach his goals only once he has ceased to value them as heavenly joys and when achieving them can bring him nothing more than middling happiness; that he feel delight only after he has become incapable of feeling *living* delights. Many experience this while they are still quite young; since their desires are slight they often manage quite well, and they look forward to manhood as a merging of wit and experience. Others never reach this stage in their lifetime; they are the few whose strength of feeling is so great at the start that it never diminishes over the years. These men would enjoy life more than anyone else, had nature destined life something to be enjoyed. But such men are on the contrary absolutely unhappy; they remain till death children in the ways of a world they cannot understand.

LXXX

Meeting again after several years a person I knew as a young man, at first I always think I see someone who has suffered some terrible misfortune. The look of joy and confidence belongs only to one's early years; the sensation of loss, along with the daily increasing physical discomforts of age, are soon felt even by the most frivolous or naturally cheerful men, and also by those who are extremely happy. It gives them that special

similmente nei più felici, un abito di volto ed un portamento, che si chiama grave, e che per rispetto a quello dei giovani e dei fanciulli, veramente è tristo.

LXXXI

Accade nella conversazione come cogli scrittori: molti de' quali in principio, trovati nuovi di concetti, e di un color proprio, piacciono grandemente; poi, continuando a leggere, vengono a noia, perchè una parte dei loro scritti è imitazione dell'altra. Così nel conversare, le persone nuove spesse volte sono pregiate e gradite pei loro modi e pei loro discorsi; e le medesime vengono a noia coll'uso e scadono nella stima: perchè gli uomini necessariamente, alcuni più ed alcuni meno, quando non imitano gli altri, sono imitatori di se medesimi. Però quelli che viaggiano, specialmente se sono uomini di qualche ingegno e che posseggano l'arte del conversare, facilmente lasciano di se nei luoghi da cui passano, un'opinione molto superiore al vero, atteso l'opportunità che hanno di celare quella che è difetto ordinario degli spiriti, dico la povertà. Poichè quel tanto che essi mettono fuori in una o in poco più occasioni, parlando principalmente delle materie più appartenenti a loro, in sulle quali, anche senza usare artifizio, sono condotti dalla cortesia o dalla curiosità degli altri, è creduto, non la loro ricchezza intera, ma una minima parte di quella, e, per dir così, moneta da spendere alla giornata, non già, come è forse il più delle volte, o tutta la somma, o la maggior parte dei loro danari. E questa credenza riesce stabile, per mancanza di nuove occasioni che la distruggano. Le stesse cause fanno che i viaggiatori similmente dall'altro lato sono soggetti ad errare, giudicando troppo altamente delle persone di qualche capacità, che ne' viaggi vengono loro alle mani.

comportment and facial expression which we call "grave" and which, compared to the looks of young men and children, are truly wretched.

LXXXI

There are many writers who at first give us great pleasure because of their new ideas and special color but who later bore us when we discover that they are imitating themselves. So too in conversation new people are often welcomed and esteemed for their manners and remarks, then after some exposure these same people become boring and fall out of favor, for whenever men are not imitating others they are necessarily—some more and some less than others—imitating themselves. Thus travelers, especially if they are good and witty conversationalists, easily leave behind in places they pass through a false and inflated version of themselves; it's their opportunity to conceal a common defect—spiritual poverty. On those rare occasions when someone's courtesy or curiosity prompts them to speak of their own affairs (so they need not invent things), the amount they put out is thought to be not their entire wealth but just a small portion of it, their daily spending money, so to speak, rather than the bulk or total sum of their money, which in fact it often is. And this belief remains intact for lack of new occasions that might destroy it. On the other hand, travelers themselves are liable to err for these same reasons, by overrating the intelligence of people they come across in their travels.

LXXXII

Nessuno diventa uomo innanzi di aver fatto una grande esperienza di se, la quale rivelando lui a lui medesimo, e determinando l'opinione sua intorno a se stesso, determina in qualche modo la fortuna e lo stato suo nella vita. A questa grande esperienza, insino alla quale nessuno nel mondo riesce da molto più che un fanciullo, il vivere antico porgeva materia infinita e pronta: ma oggi il vivere de' privati è sì povero di casi, e in universale di tal natura, che, per mancamento di occasioni, molta parte degli uomini muore avanti all'esperienza ch'io dico, e però bambina poco altrimenti che non nacque. Agli altri il conoscimento e il possesso di se medesimi suol venire o da bisogni e infortuni, o da qualche passione grande, cioè forte; e per lo più dall'amore; quando l'amore è gran passione; cosa che non accade in tutti come l'amare. Ma accaduta che sia, o nel principio della vita, come in alcuni, ovvero più tardi, e dopo altri amori di minore importanza, come pare che occorra più spesse volte, certo all'uscire di un amor grande e passionato, l'uomo conosce già mediocremente i suoi simili, fra i quali gli è convenuto aggirarsi con desiderii intensi, e con bisogni gravi e forse non provati innanzi; conosce ab esperto la natura delle passioni, poichè una di loro che arda, infiamma tutte l'altre; conosce la natura e il temperamento proprio; sa la misura delle proprie facoltà e delle proprie forze; e oramai può far giudizio se e quanto gli convenga sperare o disperare di se, e, per quello che si può intendere del futuro, qual luogo gli sia destinato nel mondo. In fine la vita a' suoi occhi ha un aspetto nuovo, già mutata per lui di cosa udita in veduta, e d'immaginata in reale; ed egli si sente in mezzo ad essa, forse non più felice, ma per dir così, più potente di prima, cioè più atto a far uso di se e degli altri.

LXXXII

No one becomes a man until he has deeply explored his own self. This exploration tells him more about himself; it determines his self-image and therefore in some ways determines his fortune and condition in life. The ancient way of life offered an infinite amount of ready material for this great experience-of-self, which makes a child into a man. But the life of individuals today is so barren of opportunities and is universally of such a nature that, for lack of proper occasions, most men die before having the kind of experience I'm describing—they die, in effect, little more than newborn babes. For others, self-awareness and self-possession usually result from needs and misfortunes, or from some great, strong passion. Most of all from love, when love is a great passion, though passion does not always take this form. Whether or not it happens early in life, or later on after less important loves (which seems more frequently the case), by the end of a great and passionate affair a man certainly knows his own kind rather well. He has had to carry on among his peers with intense desires and serious needs perhaps never before felt. He knows now from experience what his passions are like, for when one kindles, it inflames all the rest. He knows his own nature and temperament, knows the extent of his talents and strengths, and can now judge whether he should hope or despair of himself. And he knows, as well as anyone can know the future, what his destined place is in the world. Finally life takes on a new look; he sees it change from something merely heard about into something seen, from something imagined into something real. And he feels himself at the very center of life, perhaps no happier than before but in a sense more powerful, that is to say more capable of making use of himself and others.

LXXXIII

Se quei pochi uomini di valor vero che cercano gloria, conoscessero ad uno ad uno tutti coloro onde è composto quel pubblico dal quale essi con mille estremi patimenti si sforzano di essere stimati, è credibile che si raffredderebbero molto nel loro proposito, e forse che l'abbandonerebbero. Se non che l'animo nostro non si può sottrarre al potere che ha nell'immaginazione il numero degli uomini: e si vede infinite volte che noi apprezziamo, anzi rispettiamo, non dico una moltitudine, ma dieci persone adunate in una stanza, ognuna delle quali da se reputiamo di nessun conto.

LXXXIV

Gesù Cristo fu il primo che distintamente additò agli uomini quel lodatore e precettore di tutte le virtù finte, detrattore e persecutore di tutte le vere; quell'avversario d'ogni grandezza intrinseca e veramente propria dell'uomo; derisore d'ogni sentimento alto, se non lo crede falso, d'ogni affetto dolce, se lo crede intimo; quello schiavo dei forti, tiranno dei deboli, odiatore degl'infelici; il quale esso Gesù Cristo dinotò col nome di mondo, che gli dura in tutte le lingue colte insino al presente. Questa idea generale, che è di tanta verità, e che poscia è stata e sarà sempre di tanto uso, non credo che avanti quel tempo fosse nata ad altri, nè mi ricordo che si trovi, intendo dire sotto una voce unica o sotto una forma precisa, in alcun filosofo gentile. Forse perchè avanti quel tempo la viltà e la frode non fossero affatto adulte, e la civiltà non fosse giunta a quel luogo dove gran parte dell'esser suo si confonde con quello della corruzione.

Tale in somma quale ho detto di sopra, e quale fu significato da Gesù Cristo, è l'uomo che chiamiamo civile: cioè quell'uomo che la ragione e l'ingegno non rivelano, che i libri e gli edu-

LXXXIII

If those few truly worthy men who seek glory were to know
each and every individual who goes to make up the public
whose esteem they take such great pains to win, their aspirations would probably cool considerably—they might even
abandon them altogether. Except that we cannot shake the
powerful hold a crowd has on our imagination. It's so often obvious that we value, indeed respect, I wouldn't say a *mass* of
people but just ten persons gathered in a room, each of whom
taken individually we regard as being of no account.

LXXXIV

Jesus Christ was the first to point out clearly to mankind that
teacher and celebrator of all false virtues; that detractor and
persecutor of all true virtues; that enemy of all man's intrinsic
and truly unique greatness; that mocker of every noble sentiment it believes true and every gentle affection it thinks intimate; that slave of the strong, tyrant of the weak, hater of the
unhappy—which Jesus Christ called "the world," a name pre-
served in all civilized languages down to the present. This general idea, so obviously true and so dependably useful, did not,
I think, occur to anyone else before that time. Nor do I recall its
being found in any ancient philosophy; I mean in a single word
or in such precise form. Perhaps because at that time cowardice
and deceit had not yet come of age, and civilization had not
reached the point where the existence of corruption blends so
thoroughly with the existence of civilization.

This then, as I said earlier, and as Jesus Christ indicated, is
what we call civilized man. The man that wit and reason conceal, that books and educators proclaim, that nature deems

catori annunziano, che la natura costantemente reputa favoloso, e che sola l'esperienza della vita fa conoscere, e creder vero. E notisi come quell'idea che ho detto, quantunque generale, si trovi convenire in ogni sua parte a innumerabili individui.

LXXXV

Negli scrittori pagani la generalità degli uomini civili, che noi chiamiamo società o mondo, non si trova mai considerata nè mostrata risolutamente come nemica della virtù, nè come certa corruttrice d'ogni buona indole, e d'ogni animo bene avviato. Il mondo nemico del bene, è un concetto, quanto celebre nel Vangelo, e negli scrittori moderni, anche profani, tanto o poco meno sconosciuto agli antichi. E questo non farà maraviglia a chi considererà un fatto assai manifesto e semplice, il quale può servire di specchio a ciascuno che voglia paragonare in materia morale gli stati antichi ai moderni: e ciò è che laddove gli educatori moderni temono il pubblico, gli antichi lo cercavano; e dove i moderni fanno dell'oscurità domestica, della segregazione e del ritiro, uno schermo ai giovani contro la pestilenza dei costumi mondani, gli antichi traevano la gioventù, anche a forza, dalla solitudine, ed esponevano la sua educazione e la sua vita agli occhi del mondo, e il mondo agli occhi suoi, riputando l'esempio atto più ad ammaestrarla che a corromperla.

LXXXVI

Il più certo modo di celare agli altri i confini del proprio sapere, è di non trapassarli.

fabulous, that only experience in life makes known to us and makes us believe is true. And let it be noted that this general idea can also be applied in every single detail to countless individuals.

LXXXV

In the ancient writers, the generality of civilized men that we call "society" or "the world" is never thought or conclusively shown to be an enemy of virtue or bound to corrupt a good character or thriving spirit. The concept of the world-as-enemy-of-the-good is as celebrated in the Gospels and in modern secular writers as it was unknown—or barely known—to ancient writers. This should not astonish anyone who considers a very obvious and simple fact, one that can serve as a mirror for anyone wishing to compare the moral attitudes of ancient and modern states. Namely, whereas modern educators fear the public, the ancients sought it out; and where the moderns use domestic seclusion, segregation, and withdrawal as a screen for young people against the pestilence of worldly customs, the ancients coaxed young people out of solitude, even forcibly. And they exposed young people's lives and education to the eyes of the world, and exposed the *world* to *their* eyes, believing that example was more likely to instruct the young than to corrupt them.

LXXXVI

The surest way to conceal from others the limits of one's own knowledge is by not overstepping them.

LXXXVII

Chi viaggia molto, ha questo vantaggio dagli altri, che i soggetti delle sue rimembranze presto divengono remoti; di maniera che esse acquistano in breve quel vago e quel poetico, che negli altri non è dato loro se non dal tempo. Chi non ha viaggiato punto, ha questo svantaggio, che tutte le sue rimembranze sono di cose in qualche parte presenti, poichè presenti sono i luoghi ai quali ogni sua memoria si riferisce.

LXXXVIII

Avviene non di rado che gli uomini vani e pieni del concetto di se medesimi, in cambio d'essere egoisti e d'animo duro, come parrebbe verisimile, sono dolci, benevoli, buoni compagni, ed anche buoni amici e servigievoli molto. Come si credono ammirati da tutti, così ragionevolmente amano i loro creduti ammiratori, e gli aiutano dove possono, anche perchè giudicano ciò conveniente a quella maggioranza della quale stimano che la sorte gli abbia favoriti. Conversano volentieri, perchè credono il mondo pieno del loro nome; ed usano modi umani, lodandosi internamente della loro affabilità, e di sapere adattare la loro grandezza ad accomunarsi ai piccoli. Ed ho notato che crescendo nell'opinione di se medesimi, crescono altrettanto in benignità. Finalmente la certezza che hanno della propria importanza, e del consenso del genere umano in confessarla, toglie dai loro costumi ogni asprezza, perchè niuno che sia contento di se stesso e degli uomini, è di costumi aspri; e genera in loro tale tranquillità, che alcune volte prendono insino aspetto di persone modeste.

LXXXVII

One who travels a lot has this advantage over others: the objects of his remembrance soon become physically distant in such a way that presently they take on the vague and poetical tone that other memories acquire only with the passage of time. One who has not traveled at all has this disadvantage: all his remembrances are of things that are in some way present, since the places all his memories refer to are present.

LXXXVIII

It happens fairly often that vain and conceited men, instead of being hard-hearted and egoistic as one would expect, are gentle and benevolent, make good companions and also good, dutiful friends. Since they assume everyone admires them, it's only reasonable for them to love their supposed admirers and help them whenever possible; since nature has so kindly given them the majority vote, they feel it only proper to act this way. They converse gladly because they believe their name is a household word, and they act humanely, internally praising their own affability, proud that they know how to readjust their greatness and mingle with common folk. I've noticed that the more they grow in other people's esteem, the more their own benevolence grows. Finally, convinced of their own importance and convinced that all mankind concurs, they become perfectly even-tempered. (If content with himself and mankind, a man is never harsh or curt.) This makes them feel so cool and serene that at times they even begin to look like modest people.

LXXXIX

Chi comunica poco cogli uomini, rade volte è misantropo. Veri misantropi non si trovano nella solitudine, ma nel mondo: perchè l'uso pratico della vita, e non già la filosofia, è quello che fa odiare gli uomini. E se uno che sia tale, si ritira dalla società, perde nel ritiro la misantropia.

XC

Io conobbi già un bambino il quale ogni volta che dalla madre era contrariato in qualche cosa, diceva: *ah, ho inteso, ho inteso: la mamma è cattiva.* Non con altra logica discorre intorno ai prossimi la maggior parte degli uomini, benchè non esprima il suo discorso con altrettanta semplicità.

XCI

Chi t'introduce a qualcuno, se vuole che la raccomandazione abbia effetto, lasci da canto quelli che sono tuoi pregi più reali e più propri, e dica i più estrinseci e più appartenenti alla fortuna. Se tu sei grande e potente nel mondo, dica grande e potente; se ricco, dica ricco; se non altro che nobile, dica nobile: non dica magnanimo, nè virtuoso, nè costumato, nè amorevole, nè altre cose simili, se non per giunta, ancorchè siano vere ed in grado insigne. E se tu fossi letterato, e come tale fossi celebre in qualche parte, non dica dotto, nè profondo, nè grande ingegno, nè sommo; ma dica celebre: perchè, come ho detto altrove, la fortuna è fortunata al mondo, e non il valore.

LXXXIX

He who has little contact with men is seldom a misanthrope. True misanthropes are not found in isolation but among men, for it is practical experience in life, not philosophy, that makes men hate. And if such a man withdraws from society, in withdrawing he gives up his misanthropy.

XC

Once I knew a little boy who, whenever his mother opposed him in something, would say: *Oh, I see, I see, Mama is bad!* The logic most men use when talking about their fellow creatures is no different, even if they don't express their opinions with quite the same simplicity.

XCI

If a person who introduces you to someone wants his recommendation to be effective, he must leave aside your most genuine personal merits and speak only of those that are most apparent and most relevant to success. If you are great and powerful in the world, let him say great and powerful; if wealthy, let him say wealthy; if nothing else but noble, let him say noble. Let him *not* say magnanimous, or virtuous, or cultivated, or loving, or other such things, except to mention them as an afterthought, even though they may be true and most distinguished. If you are a literary man and famous as such in certain quarters, let him not say learned or profound or brilliant or masterly—let him say famous. For as I have said elsewhere, it is success that succeeds in the world, not merit.

XCII

Dice Giangiacomo Rousseau che la vera cortesia de' modi consiste in un abito di mostrarsi benevolo. Questa cortesia forse ti preserva dall'odio, ma non ti acquista amore, se non di quei pochissimi ai quali l'altrui benevolenza è stimolo a corrispondere. Chi vuole, per quanto possono le maniere, farsi gli uomini amici, anzi amanti, dimostri di stimarli. Come il disprezzo offende e spiace più che l'odio, così la stima è più dolce che la benevolenza; e generalmente gli uomini hanno maggior cura, o certo maggior desiderio, d'essere pregiato che amati. Le dimostrazioni di stima, vere o false (che in tutti i modi trovano fede in chi le riceve), ottengono gratitudine quasi sempre: e molti che non alzerebbero il dito in servigio di chi gli ama veramente, si gitteranno ad ardere per chi farà vista di apprezzarli. Tali dimostrazioni sono ancora potentissime a riconciliare gli offesi, perchè pare che la natura non ci consenta di avere in odio una persona che dica di stimarci. Laddove, non solo è possibile, ma veggiamo spessissime volte gli uomini odiare e fuggire chi gli ama, anzi chi li benefica. Che se l'arte di cattivare gli animi nella conversazione consiste in fare che gli altri si partano da noi più contenti di se medesimi che non vennero, è chiaro che i segni di stima saranno più valevoli ad acquistare gli uomini, che quelli di benevolenza. E quanto meno la stima sarà dovuta, più sarà efficace il dimostrarla. Coloro che hanno l'abito della gentilezza ch'io dico, sono poco meno che corteggiati in ogni luogo dove si trovano; correndo a gara gli uomini, come volano le mosche al mele, a quella dolcezza del credere di vedersi stimati. E per lo più questi tali sono lodatissimi: perchè dalle lodi che essi, conversando, porgono a ciascuno, nasce un gran concento delle lodi che tutti danno a loro, parte per riconoscenza, e parte perchè è dell'interesse nostro che siano

XCII

Jean-Jacques Rousseau says that true politeness of manners consists in the habit of demonstrating one's benevolence.[23] Such politeness may preserve you from hatred, but it won't win you love, except from those precious few who feel moved by the benevolence of others to reciprocate. As far as manners are concerned, the best way to make friends with men—indeed to win their love—is by showing them esteem. Just as disdain displeases and offends more than hatred, so esteem is sweeter than benevolence; and men generally take greater care and have more desire to be valued than loved. Shows of esteem, whether true or false (the recipient will believe them in any case), almost always elicit gratitude; men who normally would not lift a finger to help someone who truly loves them will throw themselves into a fire for anyone who shows them esteem. Such demonstrations are all the more powerful in soothing personal offenses, for nature apparently won't allow us to feel hatred for a person who says he respects us; whereas it's not only possible, but indeed most of the time we actually *see* men hating or running from one who loves them, even from one offering help. If the art of endearing ourselves in conversation consists in having others leave our company feeling more content with themselves than when they first arrived, it's clear that signs of esteem will win over other hearts more readily than signs of benevolence. And the less esteem called for, the more effective a show of it will be. Those who have this habit of politeness are practically *courted* wherever they go, men racing each other as flies race to apples for that sweet sensation of thinking themselves esteemed. Moreover, these polite men in the end garner the greatest praise of all, since we all feel somehow obliged to sing their praises in return, partly as acknowledgment and partly because it is in our own interest to

lodati e stimati quelli che ci stimano. In tal maniera gli uomini senza avvedersene, e ciascuno forse contro la volontà sua, mediante il loro accordo in celebrare queste tali persone, le innalzano nella società molto di sopra a se medesimi, ai quali esse continuamente accennano di tenersi inferiori.

XCIII

Molti, anzi quasi tutti gli uomini che da se medesimi e dai conoscenti se credono stimati nella società, non hanno altra stima che quella di una particolar compagnia, o di una classe, o di una qualità di persone, alla quale appartengono e nella quale vivono. L'uomo di lettere, che si crede famoso e rispettato nel mondo, si trova o lasciato da un canto o schernito ogni volta che si abbatte in compagnie di genti frivole, del qual genere sono tre quarti del mondo. Il giovane galante, festeggiato dalle donne e dai pari suoi, resta negletto e confuso nella società degli uomini d'affari. Il cortigiano, che i suoi compagni e i dipendenti colmeranno di cerimonie, sarà mostrato con riso o fuggito dalle persone di bel tempo. Conchiudo che, a parlar proprio, l'uomo non può sperare, e quindi non dee voler conseguire la stima, come si dice, della società, ma di qualche numero di persone; e dagli altri, contentarsi di essere, quando ignorato affatto, e quando, più o meno, disprezzato; poichè questa sorte non si può schivare.

XCIV

Chi non è mai uscito di luoghi piccoli, dove regnano piccole ambizioni ed avarizia volgare, con un odio intenso di ciascuno contro ciascuno, come ha per favola i grandi vizi, così le sincere e solide virtù sociali. E nel particolare dell'amicizia, la crede

celebrate and esteem those who esteem us. By joining in celebration of such people we elevate them—without realizing it
and perhaps against our will—to a higher level in society than
our own, even while these courteous men go on acting as if
they considered themselves inferior.

XCIII

Many, indeed almost all men thought by themselves and
others to be esteemed in society, are respected only by a particular group (based either on class or personality) to which they
belong and in which they live. A man of letters, thinking himself famous and respected in the world, finds himself ignored
or ridiculed whenever he's in frivolous company, to which class
three fourths of the world belong; the dashing young man celebrated by women and by his peers feels neglected and con-
fused in the company of businessmen; the man of court, overwhelmed by the ceremonious treatment from companions and
subordinates, finds himself shunned and ridiculed by carefree
people. My conclusion is that a man really cannot hope, and
therefore must not wish, to win the esteem of society at large,
but rather that of just a few people. As for the rest, he must
settle for being sometimes completely ignored and sometimes
more or less disdained, since no one can avoid this fate.

XCIV

A person who has never left those small places where mean
ambitions and petty greed rule, and where everyone intensely
hates everyone else, regards honest and sound social virtues as
mere fairy tales, as he does great vices. And he thinks friendship in particular something that belongs in poems and stories

cosa appartenente ai poemi ed alle storie, non alla vita. E s'inganna. Non dico Piladi o Piritoi, ma buoni amici e cordiali, si trovano veramente nel mondo, e non sono rari. I servigi che si possono aspettare e richiedere da tali amici, dico da quelli che dà veramente il mondo, sono, o di parole, che spesso riescono utilissime, o anco di fatti qualche volta: di roba, troppo di rado; e l'uomo savio e prudente non ne dee richiedere di sì fatti. Più presto si trova chi per un estraneo metta a pericolo la vita, che uno che, non dico spenda, ma rischi per l'amico uno scudo.

XCV

Nè sono gli uomini in ciò senza qualche scusa: perchè raro è chi veramente abbia più di quello che gli bisogna; dipendendo i bisogni in modo quasi principale dalle assuefazioni, ed essendo per lo più proporzionate alle ricchezze le spese, e molte volte maggiori. E quei pochi che accumulano senza spendere, hanno questo bisogno di accumulare; o per loro disegni, o per necessità future o temute. Nè vale che questo o quel bisogno sia immaginario; perchè troppo poche sono le cose della vita che non consistano o del tutto o per gran parte nella immaginazione.

XCVI

L'uomo onesto, coll'andar degli anni, facilmente diviene insensibile alla lode e all'onore, ma non mai, credo, al biasimo nè al disprezzo. Anzi la lode e la stima di molte persone egregie non compenseranno il dolore che gli verrà da un motto o da un segno di noncuranza di qualche uomo da nulla. Forse ai ribaldi avviene al contrario; che, per essere usati al biasimo, e non usati alla lode vera, a quello saranno insensibili, a questa no, se mai per caso ne tocca loro qualche saggio.

rather than in real life. But he's wrong. I'm thinking not of Pylades or Pirithous but rather of ordinary good friends; they really do exist and are not uncommon. The favors we ask and receive from such friends usually come in the form of words (often the most useful kind of favor), sometimes as deeds. Tangible stuff comes all too seldom. A wise and cautious man, however, shouldn't ask for deeds. One sooner finds someone willing to endanger his life for a total stranger than one who, I won't say spends, but who would *risk* even one scudo for a friend.

XCV

And men really can't be entirely blamed for this, for it's hard to find a man who possesses more than he needs, assuming that his needs depend almost entirely on what he's used to and that his expenses are usually proportionate to, sometimes greater than, his wealth. Those who never spend anything feel the need to hoard, either because of plans they have or because of future or anticipated necessities. This does not mean that such needs are imaginary, for there are precious few things in life that are not entirely or in large part products of our imagination.

XCVI

As the years go by, an honest man easily becomes insensitive to honors and praise, but never, I think, to degradation or disdain. Indeed, the praise and esteem of many distinguished persons can never compensate for a painful jibe or sign of indifference from a few unimportant men. For scoundrels perhaps the opposite holds true: accustomed to degradation but unused to real praise, they are insensitive to the former but not to the latter, should they ever get a taste of it.

XCVII

Ha sembianza di paradosso, ma coll'esperienza della vita si conosce essere verissimo, che quegli uomini che i francesi chiamano originali, non solamente non sono rari, ma sono tanto comuni che sto per dire che la cosa più rara nella società e di trovare un uomo che veramente non sia, come si dice, un originale. Nè parlo già di piccole differenze da uomo a uomo: parlo di qualità e di modi che uno avrà propri, e che agli altri riusciranno strani, bizzarri, assurdi: e dico che rade volte ti avverrà di usare lungamente con una persona anche civilissima, che tu non iscuopra in lei e ne' suoi modi più d'una stranezza o assurdità o bizzarria tale, che ti farà maravigliare.

A questa scoperta arriverai più presto in altri che nei francesi, più presto forse negli uomini maturi o vecchi che ne' giovani, i quali molte volte pongono la loro ambizione nel rendersi conformi agli altri, ed ancora, se sono bene educati, sogliono fare più forza a se stessi. Ma più presto o più tardi scoprirai questa cosa alla fine nella maggior parte di coloro coi quali praticherai. Tanto la natura è varia: e tanto è impossibile alla civiltà, la quale tende ad uniformare gli uomini, di vincere in somma la natura.

XCVIII

Simile alla soprascritta osservazione è la seguente, che ognuno che abbia o che abbia avuto alquanto a fare cogli uomini, ripensando un poco, si ricorderà di essere stato non molte ma moltissime volte spettatore, e forse parte, di scene, per dir così, reali, non differenti in nessuna maniera da quelle che vedute ne' teatri, o lette ne' libri delle commedie o de' romanzi, sono credute finte di là dal naturale per ragioni d'arte. La qual cosa non significa altro, se non che la malvagità, la sciocchezza, i vizi d'ogni sorte, e le qualità e le azioni ridicole degli uomini,

XCVII

Though it seems a paradox, practical experience proves beyond any doubt that those men whom the French call original are not rare; they are in fact so common that I'm tempted to say that the most uncommon thing in society is to find a man who is *not*, as they say, an "original." I'm speaking not of the slight differences between one man and another, but rather of the personal traits and mannerisms that might seem strange, bizarre, or absurd to others. I'd also say that you're not very likely to spend any length of time with even a highly cultivated person without finding in him or in his ways such strangeness, absurdity, or bizarreness as will astonish you.

You will make this discovery sooner in others than in the French, sooner perhaps in mature and elderly people than in the young, whose ambition is often to conform to others, all the more so when they are well educated. But whether it comes sooner or later, you are bound to discover it in most people you meet. Nature's diversity is so great that it's impossible for civilization, which encourages uniformity, to triumph summarily over it.

XCVIII

The following observation is related to the one above. Anyone who is or has been involved with men, if he thinks back a bit, will recall that in almost every instance he has been a spectator, perhaps an actor, in real-life scenes that are in no way different from those we see in theaters or read in novels or drama collections—scenes thought to be artificial, beyond what's natural, for the sake of art. This simply shows that the wickedness, foolishness, and all the vices and ridiculous traits and ac-

sono molto più solite che non crediamo, e che forse non è credibile, a passare quei segni che stimiamo ordinari, ed oltre ai quali supponghiamo che sia l'eccessivo.

IC

Le persone non sono ridicole se non quando vogliono parere o essere ciò che non sono. Il povero, l'ignorante, il rustico, il malato, il vecchio, non sono mai ridicoli mentre si contentano di parer tali, e si tengono nei limiti voluti da queste loro qualità, ma sì bene quando il vecchio vuol parer giovane, il malato sano, il povero ricco, l'ignorante vuol fare dell'istruito, il rustico del cittadino. Gli stessi difetti corporali, per gravi che fossero, non desterebbero che un riso passeggero, se l'uomo non si sforzasse di nasconderli, cioè non volesse parere di non averli, che è come dire diverso da quel ch'egli è. Chi osserverà bene, vedrà che i nostri difetti o svantaggi non sono ridicoli essi, ma lo studio che noi ponghiamo per occultarli, e il voler fare come se non gli avessimo.

Quelli che per farsi più amabili affettano un carattere morale diverso dal proprio, errano di gran lunga. Lo sforzo che dopo breve tempo non è possibile a sostenere, che non divenga palese, e l'opposizione del carattere finto al vero, il quale da indi innanzi traspare di continuo, rendono la persona molto più disamabile e più spiacevole ch'ella non sarebbe dimostrando francamente e costantemente l'esser suo. Qualunque carattere più infelice, ha qualche parte non brutta, la quale, per esser vera, mettendola fuori opportunamente, piacerà molto più, che ogni più bella qualità falsa.

E generalmente, il voler essere ciò che non siamo, guasta

tions of men are much more commonplace than we think, and
that in order to indulge in what we regard as excess we need
not stray beyond the limits of what we normally consider
ordinary.

XCIX

People are ridiculous only when they try to seem or to be
that which they are not. The poor, the ignorant, the rustic, the
sick, and the old are never ridiculous so long as they are content to appear such and to stay within the limits imposed by
these conditions; it *is* absurd, however, when the old wish to
seem young, the sick healthy, the poor rich, or when an ignorant man tries to appear educated, or the rustic cosmopolitan.
Even physical deformities, no matter how serious, draw nothing more than momentary laughter so long as one does not try
to hide them; that is, so long as he does not try to pretend he
does not have them, which is like saying that he's different
than he really is. Any keen observer can see that it's not our
disadvantages or shortcomings that are ridiculous, but rather
the studious way we try to hide them and our desire to act as if
they did not exist.

Those who try to seem more likable by affecting a moral nature not their own are making a terrible mistake. The incred-
ible effort required to sustain this illusion is bound to become
obvious, the contradiction between the true and the false more
transparent, and as a result one becomes more unlikable and
unpleasant than if he were to act honestly and consistently like
himself. Everyone, even the most unfortunate, possesses a few
pleasant natural traits; when displayed at the right time, these
are surely more attractive, because more true, than any finer
false quality.

Generally speaking, the desire to be that which we are not

ogni cosa al mondo: e non per altra causa riesce insopportabile
una quantità di persone, che sarebbero amabilissime solo che si
contentassero dell'esser loro. Nè persone solamente, ma compagnie, anzi popolazioni intere: ed io conosco diverse città di
provincia colte e floride, che sarebbero luoghi assai grati ad
abitarvi, se non fosse un'imitazione stomachevole che vi si fa
delle capitali, cioè un voler esser per quanto è in loro, piuttosto
città capitali che di provincia.

C

Tornando ai difetti o svantaggi che alcuno può avere, non
nego che molte volte il mondo non sia come quei giudici ai
quali per legge è vietato di condannare il reo, quantunque con-
vinto, se da lui medesimo non si ha confessione espressa del
delitto. E veramente non per ciò che l'occultare con istudio
manifesto i propri difetti è cosa ridicola, io loderei che si con-
fessassero spontaneamente, e meno ancora, che alcuno desse
troppo ad intendere di tenersi a causa di quelli inferiore agli altri. La qual cosa non sarebbe che un condannare se stesso con
quella sentenza finale, che il mondo, finchè tu porterai la testa
levata, non verrà mai a capo di profferire. In questa specie di
lotta di ciascuno contro tutti, e di tutti contro ciascuno, nella
quale, se vogliamo chiamare le cose coi loro nomi, consiste la
vita sociale; procurando ognuno di abbattere il compagno per
porvi su i piedi, ha gran torto chi si prostra, e ancora chi s'in-
curva, e ancora chi piega il capo spontaneamente: perchè fuori
d'ogni dubbio (eccetto quando queste cose si fanno con simulazione, come per istratagemma) gli sarà subito montato addos-
so o dato in sul collo dai vicini, senza nè cortesia nè misericor-
dia nessuna al mondo. Questo errore commettono i giovani
quasi sempre, e maggiormente quanto sono d'indole più gentile: dico di confessare a ogni poco, senza necessità e fuor di
luogo, i loro svantaggi e infortuni; movendosi parte per quella

ruins everything. This is precisely why so many insufferable people would be extremely likable if only they were content to be themselves—not just individuals, but also social groups, indeed whole populations. I know of several sophisticated, prosperous provincial cities that would be rather nice places to live were it not for their sickening emulation of big cities—I mean their desire to act as much as possible like big cities rather than like provincial ones.

C

Going back to the disadvantages or flaws a person might have, I don't deny that men are often like those judges who are forbidden by law to condemn the king, no matter how guilty he is, unless he himself has openly confessed to the crime. Although it's absurd to conceal one's flaws in an obvious, studied way, I'd praise this behavior over spontaneous confession; it's even worse when someone lets it be known that he feels himself inferior to others because of his shortcomings. This is a form of self-condemnation, imposing on yourself that final sentence which, if you held your head high, the world would never think of giving. If we want to call things by their real names, this kind of struggle—where it's one against all and all against one—is life in society. Since all men would like to knock down and walk over their companions, it's a deadly mistake to throw oneself down, or knuckle under slightly, or voluntarily lower one's head. Make no mistake: except when such gestures serve as ploys, stratagems, our fellow creatures will surely climb all over us or shove us aside, showing no courtesy or pity. Young people almost always commit this error, more so when they are gentle-natured—I mean by confessing at every chance, unnecessarily and inappropriately, their shortcomings and misfortunes—partly because they are driven by

franchezza che è propria della loro età, per la quale odiano la dissimulazione, e provano compiacenza nell'affermare, anche contro se stessi, il vero; parte perchè come sono essi generosi, così credono con questi modi ottener perdono e grazia dal mondo alle loro sventure. E tanto erra dalla verità delle cose umane quella età d'oro della vita, che anche fanno mostra dell'infelicità, pensandosi che questa li renda amabili, ed acquisti loro gli animi. Nè, a dir vero, è altro che ragionevolissimo che così pensino, e che solo una lunga e costante esperienza propria persuada a spiriti gentili che il mondo perdona più facilmente ogni cosa che la sventura; che non l'infelicità, ma la fortuna è fortunata, e che però non di quella, ma di questa sempre, anche a dispetto del vero, per quanto è possibile, s'ha a far mostra; che la confessione de' propri mali non cagiona pietà ma piacere, non contrista ma rallegra, non i nemici solamente ma ognuno che l'ode, perchè è quasi un'attestazione d'inferiorità propria, e d'altrui superiorità; e che non potendo l'uomo in sulla terra confidare in altro che nelle sue forze, nulla mai non dee cedere nè ritrarsi indietro un passo volontariamente, e molto meno rendersi a discrezione, ma resistere difendendosi fino all'estremo, e combattere con isforzo ostinato per ritenere o per acquistare, se può, anche ad onta della fortuna, quello che mai non gli verrà impetrato da generosità de' prossimi nè da umanità. Io per me credo che nessuno debba sofferire nè anche d'essere chiamato in sua presenza infelice nè sventurato: i quali nomi quasi in tutte le lingue furono e sono sinonimi di ribaldo, forse per antiche superstizioni, quasi l'infelicità sia pena di scelleraggini; ma certo in tutte le lingue sono e saranno eternamente oltraggiosi per questo, che chi li profferisce, qualunque intenzione abbia, sente che con quelli innalza se ed abbassa il compagno, e la stessa cosa è sentita da chi ode.

that frankness proper to their age, which makes them hate duplicity and be willing to tell the truth, even against themselves, and partly because, just as *they* are generous, so they believe that by acting this way they will obtain the world's grace and forgiveness for their misfortunes. That golden age of life is so mistaken about human truths that young men even put their unhappiness on display, thinking this will make them likable and that it will win over the hearts of others. And it's perfectly reasonable for them to think this way. Reasonable, too, that only long and unbroken experience should convince gentle souls that men forgive anything before they forgive misfortune; that success is what succeeds, not unhappiness; that the former rather than the latter is what one must always display, in spite of the truth; that confessing one's troubles elicits not pity but pleasure, which thrills rather than saddens others, thrills not only one's enemies but also anyone who overhears the confession, since it's practically an admission of one's own inferiority and the superiority of others. And that since man is unable here on earth to trust in anything but his own strength, he must never yield or step back even one inch, much less give way voluntarily; rather he must stand firm, defending himself to the very end, fighting hard to retain or acquire if he can— fortune notwithstanding—that which shall never be granted him by his neighbors' generosity or by mankind. For my own part, I don't think anyone should even allow himself to be called unhappy or unfortunate in his presence; in almost every language, these words, perhaps from ancient superstitions, have been synonymous with scoundrel, as if unhappiness were the penalty for wickedness. But certainly in all languages they are and always will be terms of abuse, because whoever uses them, whatever his intention, feels that with these he elevates himself and disparages his companion, and anyone listening feels the same way.

CI

Confessando i propri mali, quantunque palesi, l'uomo nuoce molte volte ancora alla stima, e quindi all'affetto, che gli portano i suoi più cari: tanto è necessario che ognuno con braccio forte sostenga se medesimo, e che in qualunque stato, e a dispetto di qualunque infortunio, mostrando di se una stima ferma e sicura, dia esempio di stimarlo agli altri, e quasi li costringa colla sua propria autorità. Perchè se l'estimazione di un uomo non comincia da esso, difficilmente comincerà ella altronde: e se non ha saldissimo fondamento in lui, difficilmente starà in piedi. La società degli uomini è simile ai fluidi; ogni molecola dei quali, o globetto, premendo fortemente i vicini di sotto e di sopra e da tutti i lati, e per mezzo di quelli i lontani, ed essendo ripremuto nella stessa guisa, se in qualche posto il resistere e il risospingere diventa minore, non passa un attimo, che, concorrendo verso colà a furia tutta la mole del fluido, quel posto è occupato da globetti nuovi.

CII

Gli anni della fanciullezza sono, nella memoria di ciascheduno, quasi i tempi favolosi della sua vita; come, nella memoria delle nazioni, i tempi favolosi sono quelli della fanciullezza delle medesime.

CIII

Le lodi date a noi, hanno forza di rendere stimabili al nostro giudizio materie e facoltà da noi prima vilipese, ogni volta che ci avvenga di essere lodati in alcuna di così fatte.

CI

In confessing his own problems, however obvious they are, a man often damages the esteem and hence the affection of those closest to him. Each person, then, must forcibly control himself; by showing firm and assured *self*-esteem, whatever his condition and regardless of any misfortune, he sets an example for others to follow and practically compels them with his authority. For if esteem does not begin here, it's unlikely to begin anywhere else; and if it has not got an absolutely solid basis in oneself, it's unlikely to remain standing. Human society is like fluids: every molecule, every globule, presses hard against its neighbors above, below, and on all sides, and through these exerts pressure on far-off molecules as well, while being pushed back in the same way; if at any point this active resistance flags, within a split second the entire mass of fluid rushes to that weak spot and fills it immediately with new molecules.

CII

We remember childhood as the fabulous years of our lives, and nations remember their childhood as fabulous years.

CIII

Praise has the power to make us feel esteem for material goods and intellectual gifts that we once scorned, whenever we happen to be praised for such things.

CIV

L'educazione che ricevono, specialmente in Italia, quelli che sono educati (che a dir vero, non sono molti), è un formale tradimento ordinato dalla debolezza contro la forza, dalla vecchiezza contro la gioventù. I vecchi vengono a dire ai giovani: fuggite i piaceri propri della vostra età, perchè tutti sono pericolosi e contrari ai buoni costumi, e perchè noi che ne abbiamo presi quanti più abbiamo potuto, e che ancora, se potessimo, ne prenderemmo altrettanti, non ci siamo più atti, a causa degli anni. Non vi curate di vivere oggi; ma siate ubbidienti, sofferite, e affaticatevi quanto più sapete, per vivere quando non sarete più a tempo. Saviezza e onestà vogliono che il giovane si astenga quanto è possibile dal far uso della gioventù, eccetto per superare gli altri nelle fatiche. Della vostra sorte e di ogni cosa importante lasciate la cura a noi, che indirizzeremo il tutto all'utile nostro. Tutto il contrario di queste cose ha fatto ognuno di noi alla vostra età, e ritornerebbe a fare se ringiovanisse: ma voi guardate alle nostre parole, e non ai nostri fatti passati, nè alle nostre intenzioni. Così facendo, credete a noi conoscenti ed esperti delle cose umane, che voi sarete felici. Io non so che cosa sia inganno e fraude, se non è il promettere felicità agl'inesperti sotto tali condizioni.

L'interesse della tranquillità comune, domestica e pubblica, è contrario ai piaceri ed alle imprese dei giovani; e perciò anche l'educazione buona, o così chiamata, consiste in gran parte nell'ingannare gli allievi, acciocchè pospongano il comodo proprio all'altrui. Ma senza questo, i vecchi tendono naturalmente a distruggere, per quanto è in loro, e a cancellare dalla vita umana la gioventù, lo spettacolo della quale abborrono. In tutti i tempi la vecchiaia fu congiurata contro la giovinezza, perchè in tutti i tempi fu propria degli uomini la viltà di condannare e perseguitare in altri quei beni che essi più desidererebbero a se medesimi. Ma però non lascia d'esser notabile che, tra gli edu-

CIV

The wisdom passed on, especially in Italy, to those who are educated (who, as we know, are few indeed) is a formal traitorous conspiracy of weakness against strength, age against youth. The old come to the young and say: "Beware the pleasures proper to your age, because they are all dangerous and contrary to good manners and because we who used to enjoy them to the fullest would still enjoy them if we could, if we weren't so old. Don't bother with living today, rather be obedient, suffer, and labor as hard as you know how, so that you can really begin to live later on when your time has run out. Wisdom and honesty demand that a young man refrain as much as possible from putting his youth to good use, except to outstrip others in these labors. Let *us* look after your future and everything else that's important; *we* will handle everything in your best interest. Each of us did the exact opposite of this when we were your age and would do so again if we could somehow win back our youth. But do as we say, not as we've done or would like to do. Trust in our knowledge and expertise in human affairs and you will be happy." If promising happiness under such conditions isn't deceit and fraud, I don't know what is.

The interest of common tranquillity, domestic and public, runs contrary to the pleasures and endeavors of young people; hence even good education, so called, consists largely in tricking students into postponing their own comfort for the sake of others. But even apart from this, our elders are naturally inclined to destroy youth, to erase it entirely, since they abhor the very sight of it. Age has always conspired against youth; in their characteristic meanness, men have always condemned and persecuted in others those blessings they most desire for themselves. But still it's remarkable to find so many educators

catori, i quali, se mai persona al mondo, fanno professione di cercare il bene dei prossimi, si trovino tanti che cerchino di privare i loro allievi del maggior bene della vita, che è la giovinezza. Più notabile è, che mai padre nè madre, non che altro istitutore, non sentì rimordere la coscienza del dare ai figliuoli un'educazione che muove da un principio così maligno. La qual cosa farebbe più maraviglia, se già lungamente, per altre cause, il procurare l'abolizione della gioventù, non fosse stata creduta opera meritoria.

Frutto di tale cultura malefica, o intenta al profitto del cultore con rovina della pianta, si è, o che gli alunni, vissuti da vecchi nell'età florida, si rendono ridicoli e infelici in vecchiezza, volendo vivere da giovani; ovvero, come accade più spesso, che la natura vince, e che i giovani vivendo da giovani in dispetto dell'educazione, si fanno ribelli agli educatori, i quali se avessero favorito l'uso e il godimento delle loro facoltà giovanili, avrebbero potuto regolarlo, mediante la confidenza degli allievi, che non avrebbero mai perduta.

CV

L'astuzia, la quale appartiene all'ingegno, è usata moltissime volte per supplire la scarsità di esso ingegno, e per vincere maggior copia del medesimo in altri.

CVI

Il mondo a quelle cose che altrimenti gli converrebbe ammirare ride; e biasima, come la volpe d'Esopo, quelle che invidia. Una gran passione d'amore, con grandi consolazioni di grandi travagli, è invidiata universalmente; e perciò biasimata con più calore. Una consuetudine generosa, un'azione eroica, dovrebb'essere ammirata: ma gli uomini se ammirassero, specialmen-

CIX

L'uomo è quasi sempre tanto malvagio quanto gli bisogna. Se
si conduce dirittamente, si può giudicare che la malvagità non
gli è necessaria. Ho visto persone di costumi dolcissimi, inno-
centissimi, commettere azioni delle più atroci, per fuggire qualche danno grave, non evitabile in altra guisa.

CX

È curioso a vedere che quasi tutti gli uomini che vagliono
molto, hanno le maniere semplici; e che quasi sempre le maniere semplici sono prese per indizio di poco valore.

CXI

Un abito silenzioso nella conversazione, allora piace ed è
grato, quando si conosce che la persona che tace ha quanto si
chiede e ardimento e attitudine a parlare.

(who in the world professes more than they to seek their neighbor's welfare?) trying to deprive their students of life's greatest
blessing—youth. And even more remarkable that no father or
mother, let alone any teacher, has ever felt pangs of conscience
for giving their children an education inspired by such an evil
principle. This would be more astonishing if the abolishment
of youth had not already—for a long time and for different reasons—been thought a worthwhile endeavor.

The fruit of such a malevolent culture, which benefits the
cultivator while ruining the plant, is that students, having
lived like old men during their growing years, become ridiculous and unhappy in old age because they yearn to live like
boys; or else, as happens more often, nature triumphs and the
young live "youthfully" in spite of education, rebelling against
their teachers. Had these teachers won their pupils' confidence
by *encouraging* the use and enjoyment of the gifts of youth,
they could then have regulated these gifts and would never
have lost that confidence.

CV

Cunning, an attribute of intelligence, is very often used to
compensate for a lack of real intelligence and to defeat the
greater intellectual powers of others.

CVI

The world laughs at things it would really prefer to admire,
and like Aesop's fox it criticizes things it covets. A grand passionate love, with its great pains greatly rewarded, is universally envied and hence fiercely attacked. A habit of generosity
or a heroic act ought to be admired, but if men admired them,
especially in their peers, they would feel humiliated; so rather

te negli uguali, se crederebbero umiliati; e perciò, in cambio d'ammirare, ridono. Questa cosa va tant'oltre, che nella vita comune è necessario dissimulare con più diligenza la nobiltà dell'operare, che la viltà: perchè la viltà è di tutti, e però almeno è perdonata; la nobiltà è contro l'usanza, e pare che indichi presunzione, o che da se richiegga lode; la quale il pubblico, e massime i conoscenti, non amano di dare con sincerità.

CVII

Molte scempiataggini si dicono in compagnia per voglia di favellare. Ma il giovane che ha qualche stima di se medesimo, quando da principio entra nel mondo, facilmente erra in altro modo: e questo è, che per parlare aspetta che gli occorrano da dir cose straordinarie di bellezza o d'importanza. Così, aspettando, accade che non parla mai. La più sensata conversazione del mondo, e la più spiritosa, si compone per la massima parte di detti e discorsi frivoli o triti, i quali in ogni modo servono all'intento di passare il tempo parlando. Ed è necessario che ciascuno si risolva a dir cose la più parte comuni, per dirne di non comuni solo alcune volte.

CVIII

Grande studio degli uomini finchè sono immaturi, è di parere uomini fatti, e poichè sono tali, di parere immaturi. Oliviero Goldsmith, l'autore del romanzo *The Vicar of Wakefield*, giunto all'età di quarant'anni, tolse dal suo indirizzo il titolo di dottore; divenutagli odiosa in quel tempo tale dimostrazione di gravità, che gli era stata cara nei primi anni.

than admire, they laugh. It goes so far that in ever' must disguise one's dignity more diligently than ness, since everyone is mean in some way and so forgiven. But dignity goes against custom; it see overconfidence, to call praise upon itself, whicl and most of all one's own acquaintances—do i sincerely.

CVII

We often talk nonsense in company just fo ing. But a young man with some self-respec different way the moment he enters public lif until he has something extraordinarily fine say before he speaks. Thus, while waiting, I to speak. The most sensible conversation in wittiest, is made up mostly of frivolous which in any case serve to pass the tim must be resolved to say things that are monplace, in order to say unusual things

CVIII

While still growing up, men take gr mature, then when they have becom ture. When Oliver Goldsmith, author reached the age of forty, he did awa He had come to despise that token been so dear to him in his early yea

CIX

Man is almost always as wicked as he has to be. A man might think he doesn't need to be wicked if he behaves nobly and justly. Yet I have seen the most innocent and gentle-natured people commit some of the most atrocious acts in order to avoid some serious harm that would be unavoidable otherwise.

CX

It's interesting to observe that almost all truly worthy men have simple manners, and that simple manners are almost always taken as a sign of little worth.

CXI

Remaining silent in conversation, then, pleases people and draws praise when it's known that the silent person has the daring and talent that speaking demands.

APPENDIX

REFERENCES TO THE *ZIBALDONE*

The following references between the *Pensieri* and the *Zibaldone* correspond to the internal pagination of the *Zibaldone* as the text appears in Francesco Flora's edition of *Tutte le Opere* (4th Edition; Milan: Mondadori, 1953).

Pensieri	*Zibaldone*
II	2453–54
V	4131–32
VIII	339–40; 1535–37; 2471–72
XII	45
XIII	60; 2255
XIV	283–85
XV	197–98; 454–55
XVI	463–65; 669–74; 1100; 1913; 2473–74
XVII	334
XXI	507–508
XXIII	663–66
XXIV	2429
XXV	1727–28
XXVI	1673–75
XXVII	1252
XXVIII	1721
XXIX	1787–88
XXXII	256; 3545–46; 3720–22

Pensieri	Zibaldone
XXXIV	3360–61
XXXVII	3684
XXXVIII	4197–98
XXXIX	4241–42
XLII	4141
XLIV	4247
XLVI	4201
XLVIII	4280; 4419
L	4481–82
LI	4058–4060
LIII	4188; 4469
LIV	1547; 4525
LV	2342–43; 4096
LVI	4140
LVIII	4037–4038
LIX	4268–69
LX	4153–54; 4329; 4508
LXI	4284
LXII	4283
LXIII	4285
LXIV	612–13
LXV	4294–95
LXVI	4300
LXVII	4306–4307
LXIX	4308
LXXIII	1083; 1431–32
LXXIV	4390
LXXV	2155–56; 2258
LXXVI	4525

Pensieri	Zibaldone
LXXVII	4333–34
LXXVIII	4391
LXXIX	4420–21
LXXXI	4295–97
LXXXIII	4471
LXXXIV	112; 611
LXXXV	611
LXXXVI	4482
LXXXVII	4485
LXXXVIII	4493–94
LXXXIX	4513
XC	4508
XCI	4389–90; 2401
XCII	4501
XCIV	4523
XCVI	4167; 4523
XCVII	4525
C	2401–2402; 2415; 2485–86
CI	2401–2402; 930; 2436–41
CIII	724
CIV	1472–73
CV	2259–63
CVIII	4525
CX	4524

NOTES TO THE TRANSLATION

1. This *pensiero*, inspired in part by Leopardi's uneasy relationship with his own father, may be applied to several other nineteenth-century literary artists; it also prefigures the current interest in psychohistory: "When Ralph Waldo was five, the Reverend William Emerson suffered a hemorrhage and died three years later about a month before Waldo's eighth birthday. Hawthorne's sea-captain father was lost on a voyage when Nathaniel was two. David Poe . . . abandoned the infant Edgar within nine months of the birth. Melville's bankrupt merchant father died when Herman was twelve. And although both Thoreau and Whitman lived to maturity in the company of their fathers, neither writer seems to have established a strong filial bond with them." Earl Rovit, "The American Literary Ego: An Essay in Psychohistory," *Southern Review*, XIV (July, 1978) 416–17.
2. Leopardi first met Ranieri (1806–88) briefly in Florence in 1827. Three years later, after being exiled from his native Naples for his liberal politics, Ranieri went to Florence again and rejoined Leopardi. For the next seven years, until Leopardi's death, Ranieri shared the poet's lodgings and looked after his health and spiritual welfare. It was Ranieri who published the *Pensieri* in his 1845 edition of Leopardi's poetry and selected prose.
3. A cholera epidemic broke out in France in 1832 and spread to Italy in the winter of 1836–37, killing thousands; in Rome alone, 5,000 people died.
4. Matthew 20: 8–12.
5. Diogenes Laertius reports that some authorities said that Thales "remained unmarried and adopted his sister's son, and that when he was asked why he had no children of his own he replied 'because he loved children.'" *Lives of Eminent Philosophers*, trans. R. D. Hicks, in The Loeb Classical Library (Cambridge: Harvard University Press, 1972), I, 27.
6. "When strong, be merciful, if you would have the respect, not the fear, of your neighbors." *Ibid.*, I, 71.

7. Tacitus quotes Otho as saying: "Death, which nature ordains for all alike, still allows the distinction of being either forgotten, or remembered with honor by posterity; if the same end awaits the innocent and the guilty, the man of spirit will at least deserve his fate." *The Histories*, trans. Alfred John Church and William Jackson Brodribb, in The Great Books of the Western World, Vol. XV (Chicago: Encyclopaedia Britannica, 1952), 195.

8. From the life of Vergil written by the fourth-century grammarian Aelius Donatus: "Much later and after the material was finally finished, Vergil read aloud three whole books for Augustus: the second, fourth, and sixth books. Since Octavia was present for the reading, she was deeply moved by the sixth book, and when the poet came to the verse about her son, 'You shall be Marcellus,' she is said to have fainted. She was revived only with some difficulty." Quoted in Paul F. Distler, *Vergil and Vergiliana* (Chicago: Loyola University Press, 1966), 129.

9. "And like a bear, let him fold you in his rapturous arms
   and his poems will choke you to death—
   worse than a bear, a bloodsucking leech
   who bites and sucks till your skin
   is an empty bag, all your blood
   drained dry.
   (Do I hear one now?
   Run for your life!)"

   The Art of Poetry, trans. Burton Raffel (Albany: State University of New York Press, 1974), 31.

10. "You ask me to recite you my epigrams. I decline. You don't wish to hear them, Celer, but to recite them." *Epigrams*, trans. Walter C. A. Ker, in The Loeb Classical Library (Cambridge: Harvard University Press, 1968), I, 69.

11. "Someone had been reading aloud for a very long time, and when he was near the end of the roll pointed to a space with no writing on it. 'Cheer up, my men,' cried Diogenes; 'there's land in sight!'" *Lives of Eminent Philosophers*, trans. R. D. Hicks, in The Loeb Classical Library (Cambridge: Harvard University Press, 1970), II, 41.

12. Book II, paragraph 1.

13. Part 1, letter 8. Lorenzo Magalotti (1637–1712) was a diplomat, traveler, and scientist.

14. This is virtually a literal translation from Rousseau's *Discours sur les sciences et les arts*: "Les anciens politiques parloient sans cesse de moeurs et de vertu; les nôtres ne parlent que de commerce et

d'argent." *Oeuvres Complètes* (Paris: Gallimard, 1964), III, 19.

15. Although it derives from *dabbene*, which originally meant "honest" or "decent"·(and when used as a noun, "honesty" or "good-heartedness" or "good-naturedness"), *dabbenaggine* has come to mean "excessive simplicity of heart and of mind" or "simple-mindedness" or "ingenuousness." Excessive goodness, in effect, becomes mere foolishness and stupidity, however well intentioned. Similarly, although εὐήθης and εὐήθεια originally meant "an honest, simple, well-mannered man" and "rectitude" or "honesty," in practice they came to mean, respectively, "simpleton" or "fool," and "thickheadedness" or "foolishness."

16. The note that accompanies this maxim in the *Zibaldone* (April 4, 1829) is: "sentent. 269; *Apophthegm. Ebraeorum et Arabum*, ed. a Io. Drusio; Franequerae, 1651."

17. "Il y a toujours dans le succès d'un homme auprès d'une femme, quelque chose que déplaît, même aux meilleurs amis de cet homme." *Corinne* (Paris: Didot, 1864), 219.

18. "Un malade dont le mal est incurable, qui peut juger son état par des exemples fréquens et familiers, qui en est averti par les mouvemens inquiets de sa famille, pas les larmes de ses amis, par la contenance ou l'abandon des médecins, n'est pas plus convaincu qu'il touche à sa dernière heure. L'intérêt est si grand qu'on ne s'en rapporte qu'à soi; on n'en croit pas les jugemens des autres, on les regarde comme des alarmes peu fondées; tant qu'on se sent et qu'on pense, on ne réfléchit, on ne raisonne que pour soi, et tout est mort que l'espérance vit encore." *Oeuvres Complètes* (Paris: Furne, 1837), III, 217.

19. "Il n'est pas si aisé de se faire un nom par un ouvrage parfait, que d'en faire valoir un médiocre par le nom qu'on s'est déjà acquis." *Oeuvres Complètes* (Paris: Gallimard, 1951), 65.

20. In archaic usage, *noia* often meant "pain" or "suffering," as in Dante's "Ma tu perché ritorni a tanta noia?" In modern usage, it denotes at once a feeling and a state of mind and is commonly used to mean "boredom," "tedium," "monotony," or "annoyance." *Noia* is perhaps the most important word in Leopardi's vocabulary. In the *Zibaldone,* he describes it as "the most sterile of all human passions. It is the child of nullity and thus the mother of nothingness" (September 30, 1821). It represents "an emptiness of the soul" inseparable from yearning and desire and the failure of huge imaginative aspirations; its melancholy is all the more painful when one recognizes the impossibility of realizing one's aspirations. Leopardi later notes, again in the *Zibaldone*, that *noia* is not a specific localized pain but that it is rather "the simple life fully felt,

tested, known, fully present in the individual, *occupying* him" (March 8, 1824). The most thorough study of this phenomenon is Kuhn's *The Demon of Noontide*, and his detailed definition of *noia* or *ennui* is worth quoting at length: "We can tentatively define *ennui* as the state of emptiness that the soul feels when it is deprived of interest in action, life, and the world (be it this world or another), a condition that is the immediate consequence of the encounter with nothingness, and has as an immediate effect a disaffection with reality. Such alienation does in turn produce a number of different effects. It can bring about, as in the case of Emma Bovary, a morose joylessness that occasionally culminates in total despair and even suicide. Or it can result in the Byronian pride of the children of the century who consider themselves superior to the reality from which they have been divorced, who sometimes, as in the case of Manfred, think themselves the equals of the Divinity. It can inspire the artist to become, like Stephan Daedalus, the rival of God in creation. It can even, as in the case of Rance, lead to the total abnegation that is a prerequisite of sainthood. Schizophrenics, supermen, artists, and saints—these are but a few of the types who people the landscape of *ennui*" (p. 13).

21. "You have so fascinated me or fired my imagination as to make me desire that my achievements should be put on record at the earliest possible moment by none other than yourself." *The Letters to His Friends*, trans. W. Glynn Williams, in The Loeb Classical Library (Cambridge: Harvard University Press, 1965), I, 367.

22. "You should dwell at length on the causes and early stages of the war, and especially our ill success in my absence. Do not be in a hurry to come to my share. Further, I think it essential to make quite clear the superiority of the Parthians before my arrival, that the magnitude of my achievements may be manifest." *The Correspondence of Marcus Cornelius Fronto*, trans. C. R. Haines, in The Loeb Classical Library (Cambridge: Harvard University Press, 1963), II, 197.

23. "La véritable politesse consiste à marquer de la bienveillance aux hommes: elle se montre sans piene quand on en a; c'est pour celui qui n'en a pas qu'on est forcé de réduire en art ses apparences." *Émile*, in *Oeuvres*, IV, 669.